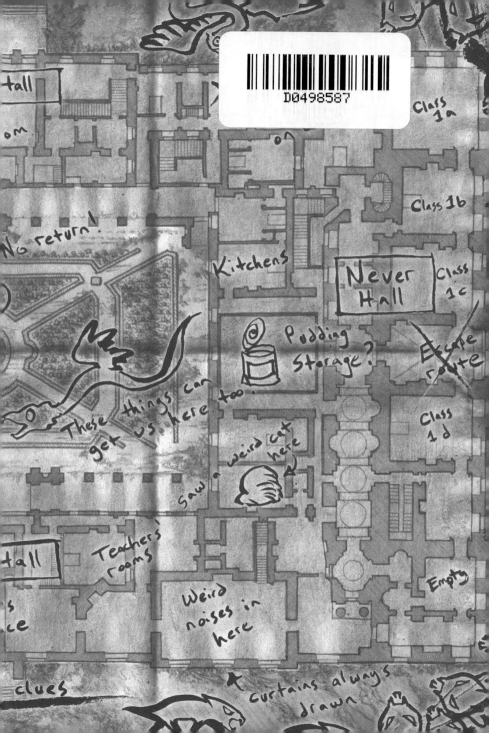

LOST AND FOUND
WITHERWOOD REFORM SCHOOL

BOOK 2

LOST AND FOUND
WITHERWOOD REFORM SCHOOL

OBERT SKYE

WITH ILLUSTRATIONS BY
KEITH THOMPSON

Christy Ottaviano Books

Henry Holt and Company ✦ New York

To those who have entered the gate and passed the statue.

It is now time to open the door.

Henry Holt and Company, LLC

Publishers since 1866

175 Fifth Avenue

New York, New York 10010

mackids.com

Library of Congress Cataloging-in-Publication Data

Names: Skye, Obert, author. | Thompson, Keith, 1982– illustrator.

Title: Lost and found / Obert Skye ; with illustrations by Keith Thompson.

Description: First edition. | New York : Henry Holt and Company, 2016. | Series: Witherwood Reform
  School ; 2 | Summary: "Charlotte and Tobias make more strange discoveries as they attempt to
  escape the sinister Witherwood reform school" —Provided by publisher.

Identifiers: LCCN 2015021508 | ISBN 9780805098808 (hardback)

Subjects: | CYAC: Brothers and sisters—Fiction. | Reformatories—Fiction. | Schools—Fiction. |
  Adventure and adventurers—Fiction. | Brainwashing—Fiction. | BISAC: JUVENILE FICTION /
  Family / Siblings. | JUVENILE FICTION / Family / Orphans & Foster Homes. | JUVENILE FICTION /
  Science Fiction. | JUVENILE FICTION / Fantasy & Magic. | JUVENILE FICTION / Action &
  Adventure / General.

Classification: LCC PZ7.S62877 Los 2016 | DDC [Fic]—dc23

LC record available at http://lccn.loc.gov/2015021508

Our books may be purchased in bulk for promotional, educational,

or business use. Please contact your local bookseller or the Macmillan Corporate and

Premium Sales Department at (800) 221-7945 ext. 5442 or by e-mail at

MacmillanSpecialMarkets@macmillan.com.

First Edition—2016

Printed in the United States of America by

R. R. Donnelley & Sons Company, Harrisonburg, Virginia

1 3 5 7 9 10 8 6 4 2

YOU WILL BE CHANGED.

LOST AND FOUND
WITHERWOOD REFORM SCHOOL

Dear Reader

Here we are. I'm so happy you're on board. The Eggers children are even happier. Your involvement adds a much needed jolt of hope. Tobias and Charlotte have learned a lot. They were mistakenly taken in at Witherwood and they almost made it out. But now they are back, stuck on top of the high mesa with a number of obstacles standing in their way to freedom.

It's important to remember that the lonely mesa that sticks up in that desert wasn't always there. A hundred years ago, a meteor struck the ground and the mesa grew up around it. Many years later, the school was built on top.

Now, thanks to the meteor that still rests inside the soil, there are many unusual things happening. Tobias and Charlotte are simply two children who have accidentally gotten caught up in a network of people who are not only up to "no good," they are up to "yes bad."

Life, it seems, is a series of losts and founds. They lost their father and found the strength to do what they needed. They lost all hope and found reasons to hope again. They lost their freedom and found a way out. They lost their freedom again, and ... well, you'll see.

It will take courage, but we must walk through that large iron gate. We must pass the weathered fountain and enter the wooden doors of Witherwood. It's strange how they arrived by accident, yet they just might be the kids to bring the school down. May you find more hope than abhorrence in their tale.

Yours in either case,

Obert Skye

CHAPTER 1

THE WOODEN WINDOW

On top of a tall mesa, in the middle of a lonely desert, there sits a school. It is not a school of great learning or art. It has no football team or even a tetherball pole. The school is Witherwood—a large three-story building surrounded by a high brick wall with a tall iron gate at its entrance. Behind the gate there are many secrets; some of the secrets are long and complicated, others are simple. Some of the secrets have to do with the students. Some have to do with the odd animals called Protectors that guard the school. Some secrets are too uncomfortable to whisper. Other secrets are noisy and deserve to be shouted. Take, for example, the secret something that is currently knocking against the window of Tobias and Charlotte's room. It's a secret that's making some noise.

Bump.

      Tobias rose from his gray cot like a baffled vampire. He had been asleep for many hours and his tongue was desperately in need of moisture. He swung his legs off the edge of his sorry bed and sat. He felt like a frog with dry blue eyes, licking his lips and staring at the wall beside his cot. The room was warm and suffocating, causing his dark brown hair to stick to his forehead. He reached with his right hand and grabbed at the hair on the back of his head. It was a habit he had had since birth.

There was another bump.

"Did you hear something?" Tobias asked his sister.

He turned to look at Charlotte. She was lying on her cot, gazing toward the one window in their room.

"I might have heard something," she croaked. "It's really warm in here."

"I know," Tobias whispered hoarsely, "and I can't remember if that window opens."

"I don't think it does."

Charlotte sat up on her cot with her legs sticking out straight in front of her like a wooden doll. Her blond hair was a mess in the back but organized in the front. She was wearing the uniform all the girls wore at Witherwood: white shirt, plaid skirt, red socks to the knees, and black flats that clung to her feet like two stones in need of polishing. Her brain was fully under the spell of Marvin Withers's mind-controlling voice. Her brown eyes were smoky and blinking slowly.

"We live here, right?" Charlotte asked in confusion. "In this room?"

Tobias nodded.

"Do we like it here?"

"I think so," Tobias replied.

"How can we like a place that's so hot?"

Bump.

Tobias blinked. His foggy mind was poking and pinching all of his senses. He looked around, wondering what he was bothered about. The room was just as it always had been. There were two rows of gray cots lined up across from each other. The cots were all empty, and a couple of them were torn up. At the end of one, there were some empty shoes and folded clothes sitting on the floor. Tobias looked across the room to the door that led to the hallway in Weary Hall. He twisted his neck back and forth and then let his eyes look up at the big window. It faced the back of the mesa, where scrubby trees and prickly bushes filled the view. There were thick bars on the outside of the glass to keep people in, and heavy green curtains hung from the sides like dirty hair.

Tobias stood up and walked to the window. He tugged on the

small lock at the window's edge, but there was no budge. The sky outside was gray. It was hard to tell if it was early morning or late afternoon.

"What are you doing?" Charlotte asked.

"I really think I heard something."

Tobias stared out the window into the gray. Through the bars he could see trees swaying and bits of cloud scooting across the sky. He blinked slowly.

Bump.

Tobias stepped back from the window as something round and yellow hit the glass and rested on one of the bars outside.

"What the . . . ?"

Charlotte got up and stood next to her brother. The little animal sitting on the bar was about the size of an orange, with feathery-looking dreadlocks. It had a small olive-sized nose and two eyes that were gazing through the glass and directly toward Charlotte.

"What is it?" Charlotte asked.

Tobias's brain was jumping up and down, trying to help him recognize the small creature they had met in the gardens and that Charlotte had named Lars.

"I don't know what it is," Tobias said. "Does it look familiar?"

"No. Well, maybe a little," Charlotte said sadly.

The little creature looked up at the sky, fluttered, squawked, and then flew off. Both of the Eggers children pushed their faces up against the glass trying to see where it had gone.

Whack!

Something much larger than Lars slammed against the bars and scratched at the window. Both kids jumped back. Tobias tumbled over one of the empty cots and fell to the floor. Charlotte didn't need a cot to help her fall. She went to her knees and then scrambled back onto her feet as fast as she could.

"What happened?"

"I don't know," Tobias said.

This time, a large red animal had slammed against the window. Tobias stood up and backed away.

"What is that?"

"I don't know that either," Tobias answered. "Maybe we should leave our room."

Whatever it was hit the window again. This time they could see feathers, and talons reaching through the bars and tearing at the glass.

Tobias spun on his heels and walked quickly toward the door. Charlotte duplicated the motion and kept in step with her brother. The feathery beast slammed up against the window again. The sound of glass beginning to split and crack ripped through the stuffy air.

Reaching the door, Tobias tried the knob, but it was immovable—locked tight.

The beast hit the window again and glass blew inward, shooting about the room like twinkling daggers. Tobias got three shards stuck in his right arm, and Charlotte's left leg got two. Both children looked at their limbs, trying to mentally digest what was happening. Their brains were foggy messes due to the hypnotic influence of Marvin Withers's voice. They could barely remember their own names, let alone how to react in such a frightful situation.

Charlotte picked the pieces of glass from her leg as Tobias did the same to his arm. With the window shattered, the animal was now frantically trying to squeeze through the bars and into the room. The children were brainwashed, but an overpowering instinct for survival kicked in.

"Grab a cot," Charlotte said almost mechanically.

Tobias reached down and picked up one of the ripped cots. Charlotte grabbed the front end of it. Charging like two rhinos with muggy heads, they ran toward the window and smacked the bars and beast with the end of their battering-ram cot. Metal clashed against metal and the sound was terrific. The air resonated with a tremendous clang as the animal screeched and flew backward.

The two children dropped the cot and stared at each other.

"Was that a bird?"

"That was more than a bird," Tobias answered.

"I think I liked the first, little one better."

Within no time the big creature was back again. It swooped down and clawed madly at the bars. The Eggers children picked up the cot and moved back a few feet. They ran with the cot and slammed the end of it against the bars again, directly into the animal's screeching beak. The creature screamed and flew backward into the gray sky. A soft wind drifted into the warm room, mixing with their labored breathing.

Tobias and Charlotte dropped the cot.

"I think we hurt it," Tobias said.

As the two children stood there looking out, the bars on the window began to creak. The damage the beast had done plus the two hits from the charging cot had torn the bars from the top of the window. The metal bars moaned as they tipped backward, away from the wall and down to the ground. A noise similar to dumbbells being dropped down a flight of stairs echoed and then stopped. The bars were gone and the window looked naked. The glass was completely shattered.

"It's not as stuffy now," Charlotte said.

Warm wind drifted in, tinged with the smell of cedar trees and dirt. The sky was growing dimmer, which meant that night was coming.

"What should we do?" Charlotte asked her brother.

It was odd—despite the fact that Tobias and Charlotte were

two adventurous and mischievous children, and regardless of the fact that there was an open window they could have easily escaped through—neither one made a move. They could have jumped from the window, worked their way to the stream at the back of the mesa, and traveled through the tunnel to the abandoned rest stop they had made it to the day before. But neither one had the desire to go anywhere. Witherwood was their home, and their brains were not letting them remember anything else. Had they been clearheaded, they might have tried to escape, but they weren't even clearheaded enough to wonder why nobody had come to check and see what all the noise they were making was about.

"Are we safe now?" Charlotte asked. "Is it gone?"

Reeeeech!

The creature swept in through the window and knocked Tobias off his feet. He rolled to the wall and covered his head with his hands as the animal tore at his shirt and pants with its talons. Whatever it was, it was wounded and angry. It squawked like a vengeful duck with something to prove.

"Do something!" Tobias shouted.

Charlotte was already moving. She grabbed two shoes that had been left sitting on the floor by some other poor student. Without thinking, she slipped the shoes onto her hands and began punching the creature as if she were a prizefighter. The hard shoes made her blows count. She hit the animal in the throat and then in the stomach. The beast looked as if it were made up of bits of birds and monkeys and dogs. It was not a familiar-looking animal. Charlotte turned and connected another punch to the beak.

"Baaaraaaaaaaafffffft!"

Tobias rolled out from the corner and kicked upward, pushing the animal toward Charlotte. She swung and smacked the creature in the back. The dazed animal wobbled and then stumbled over a cot. It fell to the floor with its feathers ruffling and its voice fading like a dying battery.

The animal shuddered and became completely still.

CHAPTER 2

CLUED IN

Charlotte reached down for Tobias. He took her right, shoe-covered hand and stood up. He was scratched in more than a dozen places and his hair was torn up, but he was okay.

"Is it dead?"

"I think so," Charlotte said.

"You're a pretty good fighter with those shoe-gloves."

The animal began to stir. Without thinking, the two children flipped over the cot nearest the animal and threw it down across the beast's body. The animal's head was sticking out, but the cot held its body against the floor like a net. Tobias sat on one side, holding it down while Charlotte sat on the other. The animal tried to struggle for a moment and then gave up. They studied its head as it was pinned to the ground. It had a long, wide beak that looked like it was covered in dark brown leather. Its eyes were bulgy and framed by bushy red eyebrows and patches of short twisted hair below. Its neck was dotted with red feathers that bristled as it breathed.

"Is this how animals are supposed to look?" Tobias asked, confused.

"I can't remember."

The animal struggled beneath the cot. It worked one of its talons out and pushed it through the material.

"Um, that's not good," Charlotte said, shaking. "Not good at all."

The talon began to rip the material more. With the cot flipped upside down and lying across the beast, Tobias grabbed one of the metal legs and unscrewed it as quickly as he could. The animal was thrashing now, trying desperately to get out from under the cot.

"Here!" Tobias said, handing Charlotte the cot leg. "Hit him in the head with this. I'll hold the cot down."

Charlotte moved to get into a better position to hit the creature while her brother struggled to keep the animal pinned to the floor. Charlotte knelt on the animal's cot-covered body and lifted the metal leg to take a swing. As she held the leg above her, she stared at the creature's head. It stopped moving for a second to look back at Charlotte. Its fat eyes and sad beak were a pitiful and confusing sight.

"I can't do it," Charlotte said.

"Here, give it to me."

As the Eggers children attempted to switch positions, the animal got a second and then a third talon through the cot material and began to rip it to shreds. It bucked its body and lifted the cot several inches from the ground. With a quick maneuver, it pulled itself out from under the cot and stood up on its two large feet to scream.

Tobias and Charlotte were on their knees, which is a fine place to be if you're praying but a tricky place to be if you need to run. They both scrambled to stand up as the animal bellowed.

"Run to the door!"

"It's locked," Charlotte reminded him.

"I can't think of anything else!"

The children turned and moved toward the door. The animal lunged in their direction. It reached out with its right arm and swiped at Tobias's back, ripping off a large piece of his shirt.

Before they could reach the door, it burst open and Ms. Gulp charged in. She was holding a long stick with a glowing bit of wire on the tip of it. The wire was crackling and shooting sparks. Behind Ms. Gulp were some orderlies in yellow lab coats, all holding sticks of their own.

"Get down!" Ms. Gulp yelled at the children. "Down!"

Tobias and Charlotte dropped to the floor as Ms. Gulp swung

her stick and connected the glowing tip with the belly of the beast. The animal screamed and lurched backward. The orderlies stepped over the Eggers children with their sticks out, pushing the animal toward the window.

Ms. Gulp took another hard swing and knocked the animal to its bony knees. The creature screamed. It was outnumbered and knew it. It stood up and, in one smooth move, leapt through the window and vanished almost magically into the approaching night.

Ms. Gulp stood there holding her stick like a sword. Her red hair, which was usually pulled back and tight, was a mess, her boxy body was sweating through her brown blouse, and her blue skirt was dirty and way too short for a woman of her size. She turned her square head and glanced at Tobias and Charlotte. She looked almost as disturbing as the thing she had just chased away. Ms. Gulp lowered her stick and took a deep-sounding breath.

"What just happened here?"

With the immediate threat of danger gone, the Eggers children's brains slowed and became dull again.

"What happened?" she demanded.

"It broke in through the bars," Tobias said.

Ms. Gulp looked toward the window. "I don't know what's up with the animals. They're supposed to protect this school. For some reason, the tables have burned."

Ms. Gulp had hurt her head in a terrible pool accident a while back. Because of the injury, she often said things wrong or got words mixed up. Nobody ever corrected her, for fear that she would berate or beat them.

"I have a feeling you two have something to do with how mad the animals are acting," Ms. Gulp said cruelly. "Things are precarious. Let's hope we figure it all out before it's too late. Now, good night."

"Is it okay to sleep with the open window?" Charlotte asked innocently.

Ms. Gulp sighed. "My life is an endless parade of dumb questions."

A few orderlies were instructed to grab some wood and board up the window.

Tobias's brain clicked and whirled, causing a question to pop out of his mouth without him meaning to ask one. "Will the boards stop that animal from coming in?"

"Who knows? If they don't, I suppose we'll have to come running to your rescue again. You two are far more trouble than you're worth. Now lie down. Your brains need more sleep to solidify the effect of Marvin's voice. Sleep, and I'll get you for kitchen duty first thing tomorrow."

"Okay," Tobias said obediently.

Orrin entered the room.

Orrin was short and mostly bald. He had four hairs that he believed were magical and could cover his whole head when combed over. He possessed a pointy chin and two different-colored eyes—one blue, one black. He had tiny feet and a warped-looking nose. He was the one who had first welcomed the Eggers children to Witherwood. He was also Marvin Withers's right-hand man. Which meant that Marvin Withers had ugly taste in right-hand men.

Orrin entered the room with two orderlies who were carrying large boards in their arms. They came in and immediately began to cover up the broken window. Orrin took a moment from supervising to talk to Ms. Gulp.

"My word, these two children have a gift for stirring things up," Orrin said, his eyes squinting as he spoke.

"That's the truth," Ms. Gulp agreed. "Nothing but trouble. They make rotten kids seem reasonable."

"They are most certainly children in need of reform," Orrin said.

Ms. Gulp glanced at the kids and then leaned in to whisper something private to Orrin.

"Really?" he asked with wide eyes.

"Really," she said. "It's concerning, to say the least. That's why we must strike while the iron rots."

"While the iron is hot," Orrin foolishly corrected her.

"Sticks and moans might break my bones, but your words will never curse me," Ms. Gulp said angrily. "I know how to talk. Now you need to know how to move it and pass that message along."

"Of course," Orrin agreed. "I'll speak with Marvin immediately after things are buttoned up here."

Ms. Gulp looked at Tobias and Charlotte. "I've wasted enough time here tonight. If I were you two, I'd sleep. We might not be as generous and forgiving tomorrow."

She slammed the door with gusto as she left.

Tobias and Charlotte stood there watching the orderlies finish boarding up the window. When the task was complete, Orrin clapped his pale hands and they all left the room, taking their hammers and nails and locking the door behind them.

The stuffy room was now stuffier and completely quiet.

"Why do we stay here?" Charlotte asked. "I think I would prefer something less horrible."

"That's the problem with thinking," Tobias said.

Marvin Withers's voice had really done a number on their brains. The window was boarded up, the cots were a mess, and Tobias looked like he had recently spent time as a lion's chew toy. Still, the children seemed okay with it all. They straightened up the cots like two obedient robots bent on making the world a more organized place. As Tobias was flipping one of the beds over and back into position, he noticed some words drawn on the underside of the cot. His brain had a hard time reading what was written.

"There's something on the bottom of this cot," Tobias said with very little excitement.

Charlotte stared at him.

"It looks important."

"Well, then it's probably best to not worry about it," Charlotte said. "Ms. Gulp told us to go to sleep."

"Right."

Had his brain been working properly, there's no way Tobias Eggers would have ignored the note written in his own hand-writing on the bottom of the cot. But his brain wasn't working properly, and Tobias felt driven to obey. He flipped the cot over, hiding the message. Tobias grabbed his pillow off the floor and moved his cot directly beneath the wood-covered window.

After a deep yawn, he sat down and lay backward like a baffled vampire who now needed sleep. Charlotte retrieved her pillow in the duck-printed pillowcase and lay down on her cot.

"Are we safe here?" Charlotte asked.

"Sure," her big brother replied.

It seems impossible, but the two children slept very soundly. So soundly in fact, that neither one heard the occasional scratch-ing outside the wooden window.

Sometimes it's better not to know.

CHAPTER 3

WRITTEN IN THE DUST

Time and sleep are two things that most people wish they had more of. How boring. I personally wish I had a dragon, or a talking cat, or at the very least a British accent. But I suppose if you are behind on projects and haven't slept for days, time and sleep would be half-decent things to wish for while you blow out the candles on your birthday cake— half-decent things indeed. (For the record, that last sentence sounds much better if you read it with a British accent.)

Tobias and Charlotte had gotten plenty of sleep, and they were trapped behind the walls of Witherwood, which gave them a lot of time. A lot of time to work, a lot of time to go to classes, and a lot of time to work some more.

True to her word, Ms. Gulp entered their room the next morning and woke them both by pinching the backs of their calves and yelling at them. Both children yelped and then immediately hopped up.

They were allowed a few minutes to wash in the bathroom. Tobias was given a new collared white shirt and gray V-neck sweater to go with his black corduroy pants and red-striped tie. The washroom was big, with large stone showers and fuzzy blue shower curtains. There were a few private stalls, and the sinks in front of the mirrors were shaped like animals. While cleaning up, Tobias looked in the mirror and was once again surprised to see all the scrapes and scratches on his body. When he turned his head, he could also see that a clump of his dark hair was missing in the back.

"I must be a rough sleeper," he said to his reflection.

After leaving the bathroom, the Eggers kids were marched to the kitchen, where they were put to work helping to prepare breakfast and then cleaning up the dishes when it was done.

Following all the work, Tobias and Charlotte were escorted to Severe Hall and to the classroom of Professor Himzakity. The classroom seemed somber. There were two hanging plants in the corners, and they appeared to have given up on life—their leafy branches hung like loose limbs spilling hopelessly from their pots. The room itself showed respect to the depressed plants by keeping quiet. It also helped that the walls were covered with a thick fabric that muffled noise.

Professor Himzakity was extremely thin. He was much like a walking stick in a tweed jacket. He also had a little nose and narrow feet to complete his all-over sliver of a look. He was a friendly man, but as obvious as his kind side was, it was equally clear that just below his thin skin there was a side of him people shouldn't mess with.

Like all adults at Witherwood, he too seemed to be hiding something.

Tobias and Charlotte sat down in two front desks. A dark-skinned student with green eyes and a bald head sitting next to Tobias spoke up.

"I'm called Archie."

"Quiet," Professor Himzakity said sternly.

"I'm called quiet?" Archie asked, confused.

"No questions," the professor insisted. "I should be the only one speaking."

Archie kept quiet as everyone listened to the professor give his weekly lesson about how important Witherwood was and how even the best of children need reform. He had a small projector with a slide presentation to go along with what he was saying. He flashed a picture of Witherwood on the wall.

"Here is the front of the school. Built from stone taken from a quarry fifty miles away. What a fine-looking institution," he said. "Wouldn't you agree?"

Everyone nodded.

"Look at the beautiful arched windows and the magnificent copper overhang above the front doors. Can anyone tell me where copper comes from?"

Nobody said anything.

"I guess we'll never know," Professor Himzakity said, having asked the question because he himself didn't know.

He clicked a button, and a new picture was projected on the wall. It was an image of the circular cobblestone drive in front of the school with the worn-down statue of a man sitting on a log in the middle.

"Once you come through the iron gate, you will arrive at this drive. Interesting, that rhymes." He stopped talking to write the surprise rhyme down. "The statue in the middle of the drive is of a man whose name isn't important, so don't think about it."

Everyone's brains were so mucked up there was no need for Himzakity to worry about students thinking. He clicked a button again and a new image flashed on the wall. It was a picture of Witherwood shot from above. The school looked like a giant rectangle with a massive courtyard filling the middle of it.

"This photo was taken from a blimp. You can see that Witherwood is three stories on all four sides and is made up of four connecting halls."

The students all smiled. They'd heard this exact same lesson many times before. It wasn't the first time Professor Himzakity had asked if they knew where copper came from or mentioned the blimp. The teachers at Witherwood seemed more interested in filling time than ever really teaching or reforming anything.

"The four halls are East Hall, which is the front of the school, Weary Hall, which is the back and the most western. Which is why it is called Weary."

Two students clapped.

"Never Hall is the north building, and Severe is the south building."

He clicked, and a new picture appeared. It was a picture of the mesa taken from a long distance. The mesa was standing alone in the desert like a large finger. Its red cliff sides were capped off by a bit of green on top.

"This is the mesa Witherwood sits on. It is a special place," Himzakity insisted. "You are lucky to be here, and lucky to have the protection we provide. As you know, there are animals that guard this place at night. They are of no concern during the day, but because we care about you, at night the doors are all chained shut. The animals don't like music. So we go the extra mile to keep things safe by having staff members sing while patrolling the halls. Any questions? There shouldn't be."

The classroom was half filled with kids all dressed in their school uniforms and eager to be obedient by not questioning.

"Now, does anyone know the meaning of the word *reform*?"

"To be given a purpose?" a short boy answered.

"Exactly," Himzakity said, smiling. "Exactly."

As a treat at lunchtime, all the students were taken out into the courtyard gardens to eat their food in the fresh air. The gardens were larger than six football fields and stuffed with trees and plants. They were the most beautiful part of the school, filled with plenty of ornate benches and patches of lush grass. There was also a fountain with running water.

Most of Professor Himzakity's students sat on the benches and on bits of grass listening to the fountain and eating the food the cafeteria provided them—sandwiches, carrots, and, of course, an endless supply of chocolate pudding. Most of the other classes were out in the gardens as well.

Tobias sat by his sister and Archie on a long metal bench and worked on eating his lunch. Archie finished his well before the other two.

"Are you going to eat all your food?" Archie asked.

"I think so," Tobias said.

"Fine, but you really shouldn't think," Archie replied. "There are some here who have gotten into big trouble by thinking."

"We don't think," Charlotte assured him.

"Do you remember when we were last out here?" Archie asked. "It was Student Morale Day. There was a parade and food. You were really interested in what I was thinking about then."

Tobias looked at Archie and shrugged. "I guess I'm no longer interested."

"Well, things change," Archie said. "I can't remember either."

Archie stood up, dusted his hands on his pants, and then walked sideways, as if he were dizzy, toward another group of kids.

"He's funny," Charlotte said.

Shrugging, Tobias picked up his cup of water. As he brought it toward his lips, his hands began to shake and the water in the cup sloshed into his face. Students nearby began to holler.

"The ground's moving!" Charlotte screamed.

She was right: the mesa Witherwood was sitting on seemed to be trembling and shaking, as if it were trying to balance on a rubber stick. Trees were vibrating, and orderlies and students were falling to the ground, having lost their balance.

Orrin stumbled by, yelling something about a mesa-quake.

Tobias dropped his cup and instinctively grabbed his sister and held her safely on the bench. Animals hidden in the trees and bushes screeched and hollered as everything tumbled. It felt and sounded like a nightmare that had come to life.

When the shaking finally stopped, Tobias let go of his sister. Students were now crying and picking themselves up off the ground.

"Everyone calm down," Ms. Gulp said through a bullhorn. "There's no cause for a charm. It was just a little tremor! Perfectly normal. Stop crying! These things crappen."

Before Tobias could get his head to stop shaking, another new set of screams shot down from overhead. Everyone looked up to see a massive red animal streaking across the sky. It circled back around and dove into the courtyard. In less time than it took to blink, the animal reached out its talons and picked up a boy by the shoulders. The boy was screaming as the giant flying beast lifted him into the air and out of sight. People were tempted to just stare in disbelief, but the screams of more flying animals scared that temptation right out of them.

Every student dropped what they were doing and ran for cover. The crowd noises were much louder than those of the beasts.

Another animal tried to grab a small boy with its talons, but an orderly threw a lunch tray at the dragonlike bird and beaned it in one of its big dark eyes. The animal missed the boy and slammed into the ground. Dirt burst up as rocks and leaves shot in all directions.

Tobias stood fixated and frozen. His body trembled as his eyes and brain tried to properly take in what he was seeing. The creature on the ground had long feathery wings and a furry body that resembled a giant ferret. Its face was flat with a wide beak. The animal stood up and shook its head while another creature streaked across the sky above.

"Run!" Professor Himzakity yelled. "Everyone inside!"

Tobias grabbed his sister's hand and raced toward Weary Hall. An orderly ran by, carrying a long tranquilizer gun. He was loading the weapon with a green feathery dart as he hollered to another staff member.

"Stop the Protectors!"

Tobias could see Archie in the distance, running with a huge armful of food he had picked up when others had thrown theirs down. Tobias opened his mouth to yell, but before he could say anything, a wad of blue feathers and limbs swooped into the courtyard and picked up Archie. The beast lifted him as if their

overweight friend weighed nothing. Archie dropped all the food he was carrying and screamed.

Tobias stopped running and bent down to pick up rocks off the ground. He instinctively threw them at the creature, but it was no use. The animal flew off too quickly and Tobias's rocks were falling and hitting other students in the garden.

Charlotte just stood there staring into the sky as Archie was taken away. The air around her was filled with noise as students ran like unorganized ants in all directions with no idea of what to do.

"Move!" Orrin shouted as he directed the heavy flow of human traffic with his arms. "Get indoors. We can't afford to lose any of you!"

Charlotte ran and Tobias tried to keep up with her. Overhead, other animals were hissing as their shadows raced over the fleeing students. The Eggers kids reached Weary Hall and followed the trail of other people into the building. As an alarm continued to ring, a voice came on over the speakers barking out orders.

"ALL STUDENTS TO THEIR ROOMS! ALL STUDENTS TO THEIR ROOMS. YOU WILL STAY PUT UNTIL FURTHER INSTRUCTION. ALL STUDENTS TO THEIR ROOMS. ANYONE CAUGHT IN THE GARDENS OR HALLS WILL BE PUNISHED!"

Tobias and Charlotte split off from those they were following and ran down Weary Hall back to their room. They were the only students in Weary, so they were now running alone. The carpeted halls made their movement sound less frantic than it was.

They reached the seventh door and went inside.

"What's happening?" Charlotte asked, her back to the closed door and her muddled brain trying to process what she had just seen. "Is Archie going to be okay?"

It's hard to be properly worried when you have so little control over your own thoughts and feelings. If you remember, Marvin Withers's voice has the ability to make those who hear it do as he wishes. He can make adults bend to his will and children remain docile simply by talking at them. Well, he had talked at Tobias and Charlotte for a long time. Because of that, they thought they were lucky to be there. They had no memory of their father, who had dropped them off, or of their mother, who had died a while back. They knew they were supposed to obey, and they believed they were quite fortunate to be at Witherwood.

It's sad what some people believe.

The two siblings sat down on their cots. They couldn't see out the boarded window, but they stared at it as if they could. Even if the boards were down, it wouldn't have been a very nice view. There was screaming and screeching outside as Witherwood experienced its first attack by the very things that were supposed to protect it.

The school was in a state of unrest.

Students were racing to their rooms, and the staff was trying to restore order and pretending like everything was okay. It was a messy time, but it was also the perfect distraction for Tobias and Charlotte to attempt an escape.

"What should we do?" Tobias asked as he sat on the edge of his cot.

"Wait for an adult to come help us."

"Good idea."

Sure, it was a good time to make an escape, but they were not in the right frame of mind.

Tobias folded his arms and sat back on his cot. He looked around the room and closed his eyes. As he opened them, something caught his attention. He stared at the wood floor behind Charlotte's cot.

"What are you staring at?" Charlotte asked.

"Just some dust. There's something odd about the dust over there."

Tobias pointed to where there had been a cot before they had picked it up and charged the window last night. When they had put the cots back in place, they hadn't lined them up exactly as they had been. Parts of the floor that once were covered by cots were now exposed, and the exposed part behind Charlotte's current cot had some unusual dust patterns.

Tobias stood.

Normally, something as common as standing is overlooked or not talked about. Most of us stand at different points in our lives. If you have never walked before, standing is a miracle. If you have vertigo and no balance, standing is admirable. Tobias didn't have vertigo, and he had spent his life walking. So standing usually didn't seem that impressive. But at the moment, his thoughts were not his own, so standing and moving over to investigate the strange marking in the dirt on the floor was much more impressive than it sounds.

Tobias stared at the floor for two minutes. He could see the patterns and letters on the ground, but he couldn't mentally digest them. Most of his brain was trying to convince him that he should ignore what he saw. But there was a bit of him—a spot, a dot, a speck—that was pleading with him to pay attention.

The speck and dot and spot combined to make a chunk of his brain that just couldn't ignore what was written in the dust.

"What is it?" Charlotte asked.

"I think it's a map."

"Who drew it?"

"I think I might have."

Charlotte got up from her cot and stood next to her brother.

They both looked down at the floor. There, written in the dust was a rough map of the layout of Witherwood. Some of it had been brushed over during the cot derby, but most of it was still recognizable.

"It's not that great," Charlotte said. "Why'd you draw it?"

"I don't know," Tobias answered. "Can you see those words beneath it?"

Below the roughly drawn map, there were three words, *Look for clues.*

Charlotte yawned. "What clues?"

"I honestly don't know."

The door to their room swung open and there was Orrin. Tobias spun around and his feet accidentally brushed over part of the dusty map.

Orrin stood in the doorway and looked at them. He was a mess—the human equivalent of a twenty-car pileup. His clothes were ripped, and he had some sort of rough, pointed stick in his hands.

"Good, you're here. Now stay put until you are instructed. Understand?"

"I saw Archie get lifted," Tobias said.

"He's fine," Orrin lied. "Stay put."

"The ground shook," Charlotte spoke up.

Orrin slapped his large forehead. "Just stay put!"

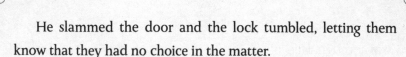

He slammed the door and the lock tumbled, letting them know that they had no choice in the matter.

Charlotte cleared her throat. "I don't remember a lot of things, but I remember I don't like him."

"That would be hard to forget."

Both the Eggers kids looked down at the floor. Most of the map was still visible, but the words were gone.

"It said 'look for clues,'" Tobias whispered.

Tobias walked to his cot, and after taking three shallow breaths, he leaned down and flipped over the cot. There, written on the bottom of it, were the words he had ignored earlier. With his brain now sparking a tiny bit, he was better able to process the information. A smile appeared on his lips. What was written was most definitely a clue.

CHAPTER 4

DIVIDED

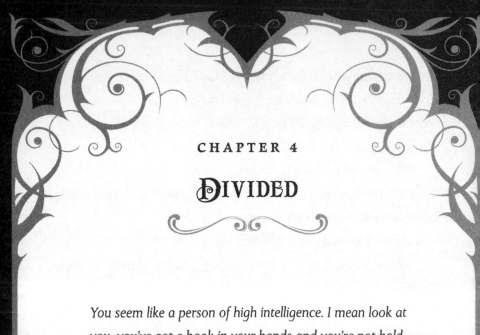

You seem like a person of high intelligence. I mean look at you, you've got a book in your hands and you're not holding it upside down. I bet people think well of you. You strike me as the sort of person who, when you're not around, everyone talks good about. Impressive. You can probably piece together puzzles quickly, solve riddles with ease, and decipher codes like nobody's business. You would be a great help to Tobias and Charlotte, what with your clear mind and amazing abilities. Sadly, you're here and they are trapped behind the brick walls of Witherwood. So the only assistance you can offer them at the moment is your sympathy.

As it just so happens, they are desperate enough to accept it.

harlotte stared at the clue. "What does that even mean?"

Tobias studied the bottom of the cot. He traced his finger along the words as he read them aloud. "Twenty-one in, seven over."

"Twenty-one in what?" Charlotte asked. "We shouldn't even be thinking about this stuff, Tobias. We should go to sleep, get up, and do as we're told."

"Maybe," Tobias said.

"No maybe. Orrin could come in again."

Tobias stood there trying to process information with a brain that had been wiped clean and programmed not to process anything.

"We should go to sleep," Charlotte said with frustration. "I can't think about anything. My brain hurts."

"Okay," Tobias said gently. "You sleep; I'm going to stare at this for a while. I must have written it down because it's important."

"No," she forced herself to say. "I'm not going to sleep. If you're staring at it, then I'm staring at it too."

Charlotte stood next to her brother and willed her eyes to look closely at the words. (It was actually a nice moment. Brothers and sisters don't always support each other, so it's worth pointing out when some do.) The words on the bottom of the cot were written in black ink.

Twenty-one in, seven over.

"Twenty-one people?" Charlotte tried.

"I don't think so. Do we even know twenty-one people here?"

"I feel like I don't know twenty-one people anywhere."

"Seven over could have something to do with hours or days. Maybe we've been in here twenty-one days and seven of them are over," Tobias wondered.

"Well, what kind of clue is that?"

"I don't know."

"You should leave better clues," Charlotte said.

"I don't know why I left any clues at all. I thought we were happy here."

"We'd be happier without clues and if we went to bed."

Tobias flipped the cot right side up and sat down on it, and Charlotte rolled into hers. There was still some light screaming and mild chaos happening outside their room, but for the moment they felt safe. Charlotte shut her eyes, and Tobias did the same as he let the weight of a heavy sleep smother him. They were both moments away from snoring when the sound of a key entering the lock could be heard.

The doorknob rattled.

Tobias reluctantly opened his eyes.

Blocking the doorway like a dinged-up refrigerator box in a

short skirt was Ms. Gulp. Right behind her stood her sidekick, Orrin. Together they were Box Woman and Bald Boy.

"I told you they were in here," Orrin said.

"Good for you," she barked at Orrin. "I'll make sure you get a glue ribbon."

Down the hallway, the sound of someone yelling could be heard.

"Let's hurry," Orrin suggested. "This is not a good day."

Ms. Gulp looked at the Eggers children. "Up!"

Both of them began to sit up.

"Not you," Orrin said, looking at Tobias. "We're only here for the girl."

A new kind of fear slowly began to drip down Tobias's spine.

"Why?" he managed to ask.

"I have no time or need to answer your questions, but if you must know, there has been a sudden opening in the girls' dorms," Ms. Gulp said. "Your sister will be moving. She'll be Ms. Ratter's problem now."

Tobias knew he should be concerned, but he couldn't get his mouth to say anything. The one constant about Witherwood was the fact that he and Charlotte had always been kept together. As horrible as the school and its mysteries were, they had each other.

"No," Tobias finally whispered.

"Excuse me?" Ms. Gulp said, placing her fists on her square waist and puffing up her face. "You think you have some say in this situation? This is a temporary room you are in now. Not many students survive—I mean, stay here long. We are moving your sister to a place where she is less apt to get in trouble. Ms. Ratter runs a tight ship. You should be happy for your sister. Understand?"

Tobias nodded.

"Very happy," Orrin added.

"I'm very happy," Tobias said.

Ms. Gulp grabbed Charlotte by the arm. "Come on."

"Okay," Charlotte said, grabbing her pillow.

"Where did you get that?" Ms. Gulp asked, noticing for the first time that both the children had pillows on their cots. She knew the Eggers kids had barely earned blankets from her, and now they had pillows with ducks printed on them. "I didn't give you those."

"They were just here?" Tobias said, almost as confused as she was.

"If I wasn't so generous, I'd rip them away from you."

"Those look very familiar," Orrin said to Ms. Gulp while examining the pillows. "Very familiar. Are you thinking what I'm thinking?"

"Probably not," Ms. Gulp said. "Your thoughts are concerning."

"Excuse me," Orrin said. "I am an integral part of this staff. I have been known to think some real gemlike thoughts. You, on the other hand, work in the kitchen."

"Well, you're a short, bald thorn."

"And you're a horrible chef," Orrin said bravely.

Ms. Gulp seethed. "Bite your tongue."

"It would be better than your cooking."

Tobias raised his hand to ask a question. Both Orrin and Ms. Gulp momentarily stopped arguing to stare at him.

"Do you think I could go with my sister?" Tobias asked without permission. "She's younger, and I think we should stay together."

"What a rude child," Orrin said. "Interrupting two adults when we're talking."

"And no, you may not go with your sister," Ms. Gulp said. "If a spot opens up in the boys' dorm, and if you're . . , well, if you're still around, we'll see about sticking you there."

"Thank you."

"Such a dullard," Ms. Gulp said.

"I find most children to be a bit dim," Orrin said. "And those children who have listened to Marvin's voice are the dimmest."

"So Charlotte's not coming back?" Tobias asked.

Ms. Gulp jerked her head toward Tobias like she was going to attack. "Witherwood is experiencing some problems at the

moment. We'll take your sister to her new bed, where she'll wait until things have calmed down. You will be locked in here. There will be no kitchen service or meals at this time. I suggest you do nothing but sleep, because we will work you all the harder tomorrow when things are straightened out."

Tobias raised his hand. "What if there's an emergency?"

Ms. Gulp rubbed her eyes. "This whole day is an emergency. Just bang on the door and maybe someone will come to your barbecue."

Ms. Gulp pulled Charlotte from the room. Before Orrin exited, he turned to say one last thing.

"Stay put," Orrin insisted. "And don't think about things that shouldn't be thought about."

Orrin left, locking the door behind him.

Tobias sat for a few moments and then stood. Yes, he had been brainwashed, but there were more and more bits of his brain that were starting to question what was happening. It didn't feel right to have his sister taken away, and that feeling jabbed his brain like a sharp, persistent needle.

Standing alone in the room, he glanced at the wooden window and the two rows of gray cots. His world was so small and confusing. He walked to the door and jiggled the handle to make sure it was locked. He switched off the yellow light and the room was as dark as tar.

Tobias hit the switch again.

Light snapped on like the flash of a bright idea.

"Twenty-one in, seven over," he said, whispering the clue aloud.

There weren't twenty-one cots, but there were definitely more than seven. The clue didn't seem to be connected to the cots. He looked at the walls and the ceiling and the floor. Nothing seemed to fit the clue. Tobias walked to the window. He tugged at the green curtains on the right side and ran his hands over the wood the orderlies had used to cover it up. Tobias couldn't decide if he should even care about clues. He didn't have to think for himself or worry, because those were things that Marvin Withers's voice had washed away. Figuring out clues often led to painful answers.

"I'm going to bed."

The oldest Eggers child was happy with his decision. It was much easier to not think about things. His bladder, however, wasn't quite as ready to settle down. He walked to the door and knocked on it for a full five minutes before a grumpy orderly opened it and let him use the bathroom. When he returned to his room, the orderly locked him back in. Tobias walked across the room toward his cot. As he walked, he realized that he was counting his steps.

"... eight, nine ..."

Tobias stopped. He looked down at his feet. A bit of déjà vu

came over him as he had the impression that he'd counted his footsteps before. He kept walking.

"...ten, eleven, twelve."

He was in the middle of the room now. He kept going, counting each step up until the magic number.

"...twenty-one."

Tobias was at the other end of the long room, twenty-one steps from the door and six inches from the wooden window. He couldn't take another step forward if he wanted to so he turned to his right and took seven. He ended up a few inches away from the wall and almost directly in the southwest corner of the room. He studied the textured red wallpaper on the top half of the wall, and the gray wainscoting on the bottom.

He looked at the floor.

There was nothing special about this spot. Tobias turned and walked seven steps back to the wooden window. He then took seven steps to the left.

Tobias was in the northwest corner of the room. He studied the floor and the wall, but like the other corner, nothing looked out of place.

"Go to bed," he told himself.

Tobias turned, and as he did, a board beneath his left foot made a low groaning noise. He stopped and held his breath. He shuffled his left foot again and the board shifted slightly beneath him. Tobias looked over at his cot. There was something inside his syrupy brain telling him to forget all this and just go to sleep—forget the clue, forget the creaking board, forget everything.

Tobias remembered that he did not like being told what to do.

He dropped to his knees and carefully felt around the floor. His fingers found a thin ridge and he slid his nails into the crack and lifted up. A small section of board popped loose. He pulled it up and pushed it aside.

"*Aaappp*" is the sound of someone with a brainwashed brain, gasping.

Under the board there was a shallow rectangular box. Inside the box there were some loose papers, and beneath the papers there was a metal key that appeared homemade and a set of pliers. The papers were all scribbled on. One large piece folded out, and there was a much more detailed map of Witherwood drawn on it. In other notes, he could see words like *Marvin*, and *Catchers*, and *Gothiks*. He had no idea what they meant. To Tobias it felt as if he had always existed in a state of blissful confusion. There was nothing before Witherwood and nothing in the future. This was how things were. Now here were papers written in what looked like his own handwriting, telling him that there were things he needed to know. There was a separate letter folded and resting at the side of the box. He pulled it out and unfolded it.

Dear Me,

At least I hope it's me who finds this. Actually, I hope I never need to find this. But if I have, it's probably because I figured out one of my own clues. There's something going on here. We were not meant to be at this place. No one is. I have not discovered everything, but I have written down the rooms and things I have seen. There is a second floor. I drew all the details I could remember about that. Study them. There is also a third floor. I don't know what's up there, but I think it's important. Stay away from Marvin Withers. He is in the square room in the middle of the courtyard. He is ugly, and his voice can erase the thoughts and personality of anyone he talks to. You have been talked to before. I found a way to clear my mind. It's painful, but it seems to work. Take a heavy object and slam it against your foot or hand. It needs to be a real hit. Just falling or getting slapped won't do. You have to trust me. Do it now! Reading all the words and thoughts in this box will make much more sense if you have a clear mind.

Do it, Tobias! Please.
Sincerely,
You

Tobias didn't know what to make of the words he had just read. It was a note to himself, but he wasn't sure he wanted to believe it. He folded the piece of paper and stuck all the items back in the shallow box beneath the floor. He then returned the floorboard to its rightful spot and covered it. Tobias's breathing was labored and loud. He didn't want to know any more. He didn't want to have to worry about things. He almost wanted to yell for Orrin and show him the box so he would take it away. At the very least, Tobias wanted to sleep so he could forget all about what he had just read. All Tobias had to do was rest his head and forget.

"Forget," he whispered dreamily.

He shuffled over to his cot and lay down. He let his head rest on the soft pillow. He folded his arms across his chest.

"Go to sleep," he told himself. "Don't think about things that shouldn't be thought about."

Tobias had forgotten to turn the lights off.

He got back up, walked to the switch, and flipped it.

Blackness ensued.

He heard someone running. There was also the sound of singing as one of the voices patrolled the halls outside his door.

"Go to sleep," he said again.

Tobias stepped carefully across the dark room to his cot. He couldn't see anything. He tried not to, but he just couldn't stop himself from counting his steps.

"...seventeen, eighteen, nineteen, twenty, twenty-one..."

Tobias wanted to ignore what he knew, but what he knew was that seven steps to the left there was a box under the floorboards filled with answers to questions he wasn't brave enough to even ask at the moment. He knew he needed to understand, but his brain was treating him like a child.

"Just go to sleep," he begged himself.

He walked straight back to the light switch and flipped it on. He sat down on the edge of the nearest cot and took off his right shoe. He stood once more. Bending over, he unscrewed one of the cot's metal legs. It was about twelve inches long and plenty heavy.

"Don't think about it," he lectured his brain. "Just do it."

Tobias lifted the metal leg up and dangled it directly above his naked right foot. He closed his eyes and opened his fingers. The leg hit his foot perfectly. The end of it smacked his toes and sent a jolt of pain shooting through his body like electricity.

Tobias covered his own mouth to muffle his scream. He shook off the pain and tried to catch his breath.

"Ouch!" he said under his breath. *That hurt.*

His voice now sounded different inside his head. The fog hadn't completely rolled away, but there were patches of his brain that were connecting properly again.

Tobias bent down and picked up the metal leg. He held it, then dropped it quickly before he could chicken out. This time the metal bar smacked him high on the foot and hit a nerve. His body shook as the pain shot from his foot to his head. His blue eyes practically jumped out of their sockets, and it took much longer to catch his breath. There were still blank spots in his head, but the working pieces were fighting to fill them in.

"I can't believe I'm doing this."

Tobias could taste the clear thinking and he wanted more. He took off his left shoe and ran to the opposite end of the room. Using the momentum, he kicked his foot into the corner leg of another cot.

Please do not try this at home.

Tobias fell to the ground, softly howling and fighting back tears. He saw stars, and stars surrounded by stars, and stars surrounded by stars that were encircled by shooting stars. As he lay on the dusty floor whimpering, the dam broke inside his head and the hopes and fears he had been previously aware of all began to flood his brain.

He knew who he was.

He knew why he was there.

He knew his father had left them.

He knew they were prisoners.

Tobias moaned.

Sometimes knowing things just isn't that great.

CHAPTER 5

CHICKEN-FRIED STEAK WITH A SIDE OF . . .

Ralph Eggers was a man with a mission. His goal was to find out who he was. Ever since he had been found wandering in the desert, his life had been one big unsolved mystery. He was currently living in the YMCA until he could find a job or discover who he had once been. Ralph had no idea that he had lost his wife a while back, or that he was the father of Tobias and Charlotte.

Mr. Eggers didn't remember a lot, but he did have one thing going for him—his new friend, Sam. Sam was a taxi driver Ralph had met after he had been released from the hospital. Sam was short, with a wide belly and thinning dark hair that he pulled back into a ponytail. He had a nose that had been broken a few times, and eyes set close together. He sometimes looked like a Cyclops. He was friendly in the sense that he talked to everyone.

He was also stubborn in the sense that he disagreed with almost everyone. Ralph had hired Sam to drive him out to the desert to meet with the rancher who had found him. The rancher, a man named Donald, had turned out to be no help. But Sam was sympathetic to Ralph's cause and had agreed to help him discover who he used to be. Sam had even driven Ralph out to the strange reform school on top of the tall mesa. It was another dead end, but a sure sign of how willing Sam was to help Ralph see this through.

Now the two of them were sitting in a diner having dinner and wondering what their next move should be.

"Well, that rancher was no help," Sam said as he waved the waitress over. "Nobody knows who you are. Maybe you were just dropped off in the desert by aliens. Do you know any strange alien languages?"

"I don't think so," Ralph said. "I'm not even great with English."

The waitress stepped up to their table and smiled a half-sincere smile. She had on a brown dress that looked as stiff as cardboard. Over the dress, she was wearing a dark green apron with at least a dozen stains on it. Her eyes were blue, tiny, and rested directly above her nose. Her nose wasn't crooked but it was slanted, running like a diagonal line from below her left eye to the right side of her thin upper lip.

"What can I get you two?"

"Just a glass of milk for me," Ralph said.

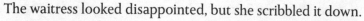
The waitress looked disappointed, but she scribbled it down.

"Something fried for me," Sam spoke. "Chicken-fried steak maybe? Is it any good here?"

"It's probably our best dish," she bragged.

"Then I'll have that and a Coke."

The waitress walked off and then Sam began to tease Ralph. "A milk? That's really going to impress the girls. Men order things that are fried."

"I'll try to remember that."

"Okay, so the rancher turned out to be a dead end, and that frightening school gave us both bad dreams. Where should we go now to find out who you are?"

"I have no idea. The only lead we have is the fact that I was saying 'Martha' when I was picked up by the rancher. Who's Martha? My wife?"

"Maybe it's your dog? No offense, but that's not much of a clue. You might not have even been saying Martha. Maybe you were just muttering some nonsense, like marfa."

"The rancher said I was saying Martha, not marfa."

"I'm just saying. I've driven a taxi for years now, and some-times I hear things wrong. I thought one lady told me to deliver her to the grave. She actually just wanted me to take her to some restaurant called the Grove."

"I think this is different."

"Still," Sam insisted. "Even if you were saying Martha, that's not much to go on."

The waitress and her slanted nose came back. She set Sam's Coke down and handed him a straw. She turned to Ralph. "I'm sorry, sir, but we're out of milk. Is there something else I can get you?"

There was an entire list of things that Ralph would have liked: his memory, his past, his name, and his family—if he had one—just to list a few.

"I guess I'll have water."

The waitress smiled as if Ralph had just made a very important decision. She then stepped away to fetch the water.

"Can I tell you something?" Sam asked. He kept talking instead of waiting for an answer. "Maybe it's an okay thing you can't remember who you are. We've all got baggage we should probably forget. I know it ain't easy, but I could help you get a cab to drive and you could run your own business here in town for a while. See if any memories come back. If nothing comes back to you, at least you got a new life and a little business."

"You've already been too kind to me."

Ralph was a tall man, but as he sat hunched over in the diner booth, he seemed small. His dark hair and brown eyes matched the coffee in the cups most of the patrons were sipping. Ralph rubbed his chin and exhaled.

"I'll tell you when I've been too kind," Sam insisted. "You should settle down and see what settles over you."

"You're probably right," Ralph said. "I just feel like I should search a little more."

Sam grumbled. "I'm up for adventure, but we haven't got a place to look. Even if you called every Martha in the phone book, I doubt that would help. Besides, it might be a Martha who lives in another country, or as I was saying before, maybe Martha's a dog."

"I don't think I would be wandering the desert calling for a dog."

"I think that's very possible," Sam said. "I know a lot of animals I'd rather look for than people."

The waitress was back. She set a skinny glass of water near Ralph and put a wide platter of food in front of Sam.

"The plate's very hot," she announced. "Chicken-fried steak and a side of gravy."

Ralph gazed at Sam's food as the waitress walked off. Steam was rising from the meal like clear worms wriggling in the air. Sam picked up the white country gravy and poured it slowly over his chicken-fried steak. Ralph couldn't take his eyes off the food.

"You want some?" Sam asked. "I'm not happy to share, but I'm willing."

Ralph blinked twice.

"Seriously, I can cut you off a piece."

"That's okay," Ralph said. "There's just something about that gravy."

"Really? Maybe it wasn't Martha you were saying in the desert." Sam put a huge piece of gravy-covered meat in his mouth. "Maybeitwahsgravee."

"What?" Ralph asked.

Sam finished chewing and swallowed. "Maybe it was gravy you were calling for instead of Martha."

"Gravy," Ralph said, listening to the word as he said it. "Do you think it could mean something?"

"It means you're hungry." Sam cut off part of his fried steak and slid it onto one of the small extra plates on the table. "Here."

Ralph pulled the plate over and picked up a set of utensils. He took a gravy-covered bite of meat and then stopped to think about it. Sam made no stops to think as he devoured his portion.

"For some reason, this gravy is making me think," Ralph said.

"I'm pretty sure Einstein always had a big bowl of gravy before he did his best pondering," Sam said. "It's just gravy, my friend, or maybe that's her last name. We should be looking for Martha Gravy."

"No, but there's a story about gravy that I think I remember," Ralph said.

"Hansel and Gravy?" Sam guessed.

"Funny. No, there was something wrong with the gravy."

"There's nothing wrong with gravy," Sam said, licking his lips. "Lumpy or smooth, it's pretty much the perfect food."

"Lumpy," Ralph said. "Something about lumpy."

"Maybe that's your name?" Sam suggested. "We still haven't figured out what it is. Maybe you're Lumpy."

Ralph laughed, but he wasn't really listening any longer. He chewed slowly as he finished the rest of his food in silence and in thought.

CHAPTER 6

THINKING OUTSIDE THE FOG

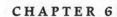

I don't want to shock you, but I believe people should think and act for themselves. I know, it's a crazy idea, but I feel like the best way for someone to go through life is for them to make their own moves. Sure, it might be wise to let the doctor perform the surgery on you instead of you trying to do it yourself. And, yes, it's probably a good idea to allow actual police officers to pull people over. That's not your job. But most things in life can be decided upon and carried out by you. Walk to the beach and see the ocean, start a small business that makes clothing for squirrels, draw a watch on your wrist and pretend that it's real. Go ahead. You're in control.

It's a good feeling to think for yourself.

Tobias, however, was not feeling good. His mind was clearing up, but the memories rushing in were difficult to view. He could remember being dropped off at Witherwood in the rain by his own father. He could remember escaping and being dragged back to Witherwood by Sherriff Pidge. He could remember being in the square room with his sister and seeing his father behind the mirror. He could remember his father looking at them like he had no idea who they were.

Tobias could remember a lot of sad things.

He also recalled a few things that were worth thinking about. He could remember some of the secret passages that were hidden behind the walls in Witherwood. He could remember his ability to draw things and pick locks.

He could remember Fiddle.

Fiddle was a direct descendant of Hyrum Withers, the founder of the school. Fiddle was a bit strange, but he was kind and had been the one to show them a way out of the school and off the mesa. Fiddle's room was also just two doors down from where Tobias now lay.

He breathed in through his nose. With a clear head, his super smelling sense seemed stronger than ever. He could smell the dust in the room and the soap he had used to wash his hands earlier. He could also smell the trees outside.

After going through the papers beneath the loose floorboards a few times, Tobias took a moment to think. He had read every word and studied every drawing he had put there. Out of all the information, what stood out most was something that was written on the last piece of paper.

Find out what's on the third floor.

He knew something sordid was underfoot. He knew there were things called Catchers that played a role in bringing children to Witherwood. He knew that there were experiments going on. The odd animals that roamed the top of the mesa were the result of some experiments. He knew a lot, but he also understood that what was most important was for him to . . .

Find out what's on the third floor.

Tobias tried to use the homemade key he found in the box to open his bedroom door, but it didn't work.

He vaguely remembered Ms. Gulp changing the locks to keep him and his sister in their place. With his mind operating better, he was much more concerned about Charlotte. She had been taken to the girls' dorms, and he had no idea if she was okay.

"I've got to get out of this room," he challenged himself.

Not certain about the time of day, Tobias tried to find some hint of light through the cracks between the boards on the window. But the orderlies had covered it so well there wasn't even a sliver of light peeking through.

He tried the door again, searching for any weakness or way to break the hinges or lock. A thought occurred to him—he had never tried beating his way out. So he stepped across the room to retrieve the metal leg he had previously dropped on his foot. He picked it up and brought it over to the door. Lifting the leg, he prepared to swing at the knob.

"One, two . . ."

A second before he swung, there was a very soft knock and Tobias looked down to see a yellow piece of paper slip quietly under the door.

Stepping back a couple of feet, he stared at the piece of paper. He set the bar down on the closest cot and cautiously returned to the door. The yellow paper was sticking about six inches into the room. It had some words on it that were small and messy. Tobias bent down and picked it up. The note read,

You are needed in the kitchen, now. Ms. Gulp

Tobias couldn't remember ever being instructed by note. Ms. Gulp liked to scream her orders, or forcefully knock them into him. Besides, the instructions were extra ridiculous because Tobias was locked in his room. There was no way out and it didn't seem possible for someone—even someone as crazy as Ms. Gulp—to expect him to beat down the door. Fortunately, being trapped was a problem Tobias didn't have to worry about for long.

The door clicked and slowly creeped open an inch.

Tobias stepped so far back his backside was almost touching the wooden window on the opposite side of the room. The door was open no more than an inch, and it was eerily silent. All he could see through the gap in the door was darkness. The halls were not lit up like usual. He looked at the note again. He smelled it to see if that would tell him anything. It didn't. Tobias put his shoes back on and moved toward the door. He folded the note and slipped it into his back pocket. When he reached the door, he flipped off the lights in his room. With them off, the hall looked even darker, but there was a gray hue in the distance.

Tobias wanted to ignore the note. He wanted to set off and find Fiddle and Charlotte and a way out. But he realized that in order to have an advantage, he needed to pretend he was still under the spell of Marvin's voice. If it was discovered that he had a clear mind, he would be dragged to the square room and brainwashed again.

And if that happened, he would be back in the same useless spot he was in before. Sure, he had found the clues to get out of the spell this time, but there was no guarantee he would figure it out again. And with each talking-to, his brain became dimmer and dimmer.

"Go to the kitchen," he whispered to himself.

Weary Hall was as unsettling as usual. It was not like Ms. Gulp to ask him to come to the kitchen this way. Tobias knew it wasn't right, but he had no other course of action to take. His feet stepped noiselessly on the carpet as he walked straight down the middle of the hall. He passed a set of stairs going up to the second floor. Memories of the brief time he and Charlotte had been up there filled his mind. He remembered the orderly walking past them as they hid. He also remembered the familiar song the orderly had been singing.

There is no up, and there's no down.
The world may stop from spinning round.
Tomorrow there'll be light, they say,
So rest up now, and we will see.

Tobias whispered the words to himself as he walked. The song was one that his mother had often sung to him and Charlotte before she died. Feelings of sadness washed over him, mixing with his anxiety and fear.

"How can this get any worse?" he whispered to himself.

You should never ask questions that you don't want the answers to.

Tobias smelled something new behind him. As he spun around, a bag was thrown over his head, turning the dark to darker. He moved to struggle, but there were two people at his sides holding his arms tightly.

"What—?" he tried to ask.

"Sorry," a voice interrupted.

Tobias felt a blow to his head and the darker turned to darkest.

CHAPTER 7

A Girl Named Sue

Here's why I don't like waking up— Well, that list is too long. Here's why I don't like sleeping in: I've got nothing. Sleeping in is one of the great joys in life. Everything is better if it ends with a good night's sleep. You traveled to the moon and back? I bet that's great, but it's even better if you get to sleep in the next morning. You just became president? Super. Even super-duper if you get to sleep in the next day. You found a cure for every imaginable illness ever? Hooray. Still, such a discovery is much better if you can sleep in on it.

Excuse me while I don't set my alarm.

harlotte was in a tough spot. But while in that tough spot, at least she had gotten a lot of sleep. She had been taken to the girls' dorm by Ms. Gulp and turned over to an uptight woman named Ms. Ratter. Ms. Ratter was like a goth version of Ms. Gulp. Her hair was black and worn in a severe bun. Her eyes were dark and her skin was pale. She wore bright red lipstick and the Witherwood brown blouse and blue skirt. Ms. Ratter was one of the more important people at Witherwood. She oversaw the girls' dorm and did a fair amount of the administrative work at the school.

Ms. Ratter had promptly taken Charlotte from Ms. Gulp and dropped her off at her new bed. She was assigned to the top bunk, above a girl named Sue.

The girls' dorms were partially open, with two rows of bunk beds running the entire length of the room. In between the beds, there were long dressers with drawers and wicker baskets on top. Charlotte's bunk was in the corner of the big dorm room, near the bathroom.

Due to all the commotion and trouble the mesa-quake and animals had caused, the girls were instructed to stay in their beds until further notice. They were only allowed to leave for supervised washroom breaks. Charlotte was okay with that. She liked sleep. So she slept the rest of the day and into the beginning of the night. When she woke up and rolled over, she nearly fell out of bed.

"Careful," someone said from the bed down below her.

Charlotte grabbed the edge of the bed frame. She looked down at the bed below and the girl sitting on it.

"I'm Sue," the girl said, gazing up.

Charlotte smacked her lips. "I'm ... Charlotte, and I'm thirsty."

"There's water on the dresser."

Charlotte slid off the bunk bed and walked over to a tall, ornate dresser. Sitting on top was a pitcher filled with water. Next to the pitcher were some tiny paper cups. Charlotte poured herself a drink and gulped it down. She poured another, and another, and another, and just one more.

"Water's great, isn't it?" Sue said.

"It is," Charlotte agreed.

Sue was sitting up in her bed. She was doing something with her hands, but she scooted over to make some space for Charlotte.

"Do you like your new bed?" Sue asked, folding a little piece of paper.

Charlotte nodded. Sue looked up from what she was folding.

"You have pointed ears."

Charlotte reached up and touched her own ears.

"We're really lucky to be so close to the bathroom," Sue said.

Charlotte yawned twice. "I guess so."

"We can use the bathroom whenever we want. Plus, we get to wave at all the students who are walking by to use it."

"That is nice," Charlotte agreed. "What are you doing?"

"Folding paper," Sue said. "There's a fancy name for it, but I can't remember what. Look, I made a frog."

Sue held up a little paper frog. It was no bigger than a small rubber ball. She set it on her lap and then pressed down on the tiny back of the frog. When she let go, the little frog flew up and hit the dresser, near the pitcher of water.

"Are you allowed to do that?" Charlotte asked.

"No one said I couldn't," Sue said with a worried voice. "I found the paper just lying around. Do you want me to teach you?"

Charlotte wanted that more than anything, but she couldn't get her voice to say it.

Sue handed Charlotte a small piece of paper and told her to copy what she did. Charlotte did exactly as she was shown.

"Don't you love it here?" Sue said as she folded.

Charlotte nodded.

"We are lucky to be getting such a wonderful education."

Charlotte was a smart child. She was kind and brilliant and clever. She was quick to care for others, and passionate about things being fair. She spoke her mind and had no problem playing the part of someone mischievous. All that's true, but Charlotte wasn't Charlotte at the moment. Her brain was a happy, gooey sphere. She didn't even remember Tobias. All she could think about was how happy she was to be at Witherwood and making a frog.

"We are lucky," Charlotte agreed.

"The girl who used to have your bed was named Kristin. She had curly hair."

"Where'd she go?"

"I don't know," Sue said, still folding. "She really liked it here, so she probably just moved to a new room. I know she wouldn't want to leave."

"Who would?" Charlotte asked.

Sue almost giggled.

"I'm hungry," Charlotte said.

"Ms. Ratter will let us know when we can eat."

"I hope she tells me to eat soon."

"She's really strict," Sue said, as if that were a positive thing.

Charlotte finished her first little frog. It wasn't great, but it wasn't embarrassing. She set it on her knee and pushed down on its paper back. When she let go, it sprang up and landed in the pitcher of water on the dresser.

"You're very good at this," Sue said sincerely.

Charlotte got a second piece of paper and then climbed back up to the top bunk and lay down.

"Oh," Sue said from below. "One last thing. Ms. Ratter said that if anything breaks in through the windows, we're supposed to hide under our bunks. They'll let us know when it's safe to come out."

Charlotte's eyes widened.

"Isn't it nice to have someone tell us what to do?" Sue whispered.

Charlotte began to fold.

CHAPTER 8

THE RESISTANCE

Tobias was trying hard not to panic. He was worried about a number of things, but his most pressing problem had to do with the fact that he had a sack that smelled like wool over his head and he was tied to a chair of some sort near something loud and hissing. Tobias shook and struggled to get free.

"Don't worry," a voice said. "We'll untie you."

"Who are you?" Tobias asked, trying to sound dim.

"We'll tell you when we're ready."

Tobias could hear multiple voices whispering. One was a girl, and there were at least two guys.

"We need to ask you some questions," a high-pitched male voice said. "For starters, what do you think about Witherwood?"

"Witherwood?" Tobias replied, sounding dumb, and scared

that he might get in more trouble if he was truthful. "Who are you?"

"Just let us know if you like it here," the girl voice asked.

"What do you mean by here? Do I like being tied up here in this hot room? No. Do I like being here at Witherwood? Well . . . Do you?"

Tobias could hear more whispering. Then, with a yank, the bag was pulled off his head. As his eyes adjusted, Tobias could see he was in some sort of big, dark boiler room. The room was dimly lit with one small orange bulb that hung naked above them. It was also filled with metal tanks and rusted pipes that ran across the ceiling and down the walls like metallic veins. There was a black door to the right, and the floor was covered with soot and grime. Next to Tobias was a large metal tank that was burping and chuffing and acting quite similar to a fat man at the end of a long race. Tobias looked down at the chair he was tied to and tried one more time to pull himself free.

It didn't work.

In front of Tobias were three kids—two boys and a girl. All three of them were sitting on wooden crates and appeared to be around his age. The girl looked skeptical and had piercing green eyes that shone even in the dim light. One of the boys was short with spiky red hair and thick glasses. The other boy looked tall even when sitting. He had blond hair, a slight build, and something to say.

"You can see us now," he said informatively. "We're students just like you. Only we don't want to be here. So, how do *you* feel about Witherwood?"

"I don't know what you mean," Tobias said, scared to trust anyone.

"He's still foggy," one of the boys said. "Let me hit him this time."

"Wait!" Tobias insisted. "Do you work for Orrin?"

Two of them spit as if disgusted.

"We loathe Orrin," the girl said. "You may not trust us, but we're just like you. Only we found a way to overcome Marvin's voice. Now, how do you feel about Witherwood?"

All three of them stared at Tobias. He looked at their faces and studied their clear eyes. It was a risk, but he wanted to take it.

"It's an awful place," Tobias whispered. "There is something sinister going on here. I would do almost anything to get me and my sister out of here."

The three kids smiled.

"His head's clear," the girl said. "Sorry about tying you up. We had to make sure your mind was clear before we let you loose."

"Is that why you hit me?" Tobias asked angrily.

"That's why she hit you," the short redheaded boy said, untying the ropes around Tobias's hands. "Plus, she likes to hit things."

"Thanks, but you didn't have to. My mind was already clear." Tobias rubbed both his wrists. "I figured out how to clear my brain by myself."

"Let me guess," the tall one said. "You left yourself notes telling yourself how to do it."

"That's right." Tobias did not feel as brilliant as he once had. "Who are you guys anyway?"

"My name's Patrick," the tall boy said. "This is Keith and she's Meghan. We're some of the few who have figured out what's going on here, and we're fighting to find a way out. No one ever comes to this room, so we meet here when we can. Our group doesn't really have a name. Meghan suggested we call ourselves the Resistance, but Keith doesn't like that."

"I don't." Keith pushed his glasses back up with his right thumb. "I think it lacks originality."

"It's a good name," she argued. Meghan was wearing her school uniform and had long dark curly hair tied back behind her head. She had a big nose and polished black shoes. She also had no problem speaking her mind. "Besides, the Resistance is much better than your suggestion."

"I was just joking about that one," Keith said.

"Still, the Witherwon'ts is lame."

"Listen," Tobias said. "I don't care what you call yourselves. I'm just happy there are others."

"Yes," Patrick said, sniffing. "It's not unusual to have a student accidentally smack into a wall or have a heavy object drop on their toes. The problem is that they usually give themselves away, and then they are quickly dragged to the square room to listen to Marvin speak again."

All four children shivered.

"Some of the students have been so brainwashed that even a brick to the stomach wouldn't shake them out of the spell," Meghan added. "There could be others with clear minds, but we have to be careful when we reveal ourselves. We don't usually go around hitting people, plus it doesn't always work. We found that out the hard way once."

"Yeah, we did," Keith said with a crooked smile. "Poor kid."

"So at the moment, this little group is all we have," Patrick explained.

"Wait," Keith said seriously, lifting his hands so Tobias could see his palms. "Hold on a second. Before we say any more, I think there's something you need to know about this group, and that is we all kind of have our thing. You're not funny, are you?"

"It depends," Tobias answered.

"Well, then you're not in this group, because I'm kind of the funny one. Right, guys? I mean if something funny happens, it's usually because of me."

"Sure, Keith," Meghan said sarcastically. "You're funny, Patrick's smart, and I'm resourceful."

"So what are you?" Keith asked Tobias.

"I'm the one who will stop at nothing to get out of here," he answered.

"Wait," Keith said in awe. "I think I wanna be that one."

"That's not important right now," Patrick said. "What's important is that we know what you did, Tobias. We know you made it out two days ago and that you were brought back. Nobody's ever done that."

"That's not true," Meghan said. "There's someone besides him who made it out."

"We don't know that for sure," Keith challenged.

"Well, he's not here, is he?" Meghan argued.

"Who is she talking about?" Tobias asked.

"His name is Andy," Patrick answered. "He was sort of our leader. He thought he found a way out. He said he would get help and come back for us, but that was over two months ago."

"How did he get out?"

"There are deliveries here," Patrick explained. "A couple of times a month, trucks come through the front gate and drop off food and other things. Andy slipped into one of the empty crates, and they hauled it out."

"And he never came back," Keith said dramatically. "He's free and we're stuck here."

"Be quiet, Keith," Meghan insisted. "You're not being very funny right now. You're sort of being the dork of the group. Andy will be back with others. He wouldn't leave us."

Patrick held up his hands to stop Meghan and Keith from arguing. He looked at Tobias. "How did you get caught when you escaped?"

"We found a tunnel that takes you down and off the mesa. It leads to an abandoned rest stop. We made it there but got picked up by a cop who we thought would save us. It turned out he was working for Witherwood. I don't know how anyone can get away from this place if the police are working for them."

"It's worse than that," Patrick said, sniffing.

"Do you have allergies?" Tobias asked.

"Nah," Keith answered for him. "He's just always sniffing, and when you offer him a tissue, he freaks."

"I don't need a tissue," Patrick insisted. "Sometimes my nose gets runny."

"Can we not talk about runny noses for once?" Meghan begged.

"Of course." Patrick sniffed. "How much do you know about this school, Tobias?"

"I know a little. I know there are people called Catchers and something called Gothiks."

Patrick nodded. "You learn things fast. Here's what *we* know. We think there are Catchers scattered all over the world. They are disguised as ordinary people who find the right kids and bring them to Witherwood. The Gothiks you mentioned are stores of some sort—secret places around the world where super-rich people shop for things that are illegal and expensive—things that this place provides." Patrick took a moment to sniff before he continued. "Witherwood must take something from us and then sell it in these Gothiks. Of course, Keith thinks they just ship kids off to work in factories."

"Like human robots," Keith said, swinging his arms in robot fashion.

Meghan shook her head. "I think it has something to do with science and experiments. Have you seen the animals here? The Protectors? Something's not right. We've gotten pretty good at sneaking around and avoiding the singing voices, but we don't know where to look for answers. We've tried to get into the square room, but at night the Protectors are out and the building is locked up."

"Have you been on the third floor?" Tobias asked.

All three said no.

"Andy's been on the second floor," Meghan bragged. "He said it looks like a hospital."

"I've been there too. And it does look and smell like a hospital. My sister and I found a way up, and we did a little exploring before they noticed we were missing."

"I remember that night," Keith said, his glasses slipping down his nose as he spoke. "They were searching the whole school for you, and they made us all lie still in our beds like robots."

"Robots don't sleep," Meghan said, disgusted.

"Sleep robots do," Keith argued.

Tobias wanted to talk about something besides sleep robots. "What about my sister, Charlotte? They took her to the girls' dorm because there was an empty bed."

"She's probably okay for the moment," Meghan said. "I sleep in the dorms. Who we should worry about is the girl she replaced. Students go missing all the time."

"Maybe they escape," Tobias offered.

Meghan smiled. "That's a nice thought, but I don't think that's what's happening."

"Maybe they get picked up and carried off like Archie was," Tobias said grimly.

"Don't worry," Patrick said, as if that was actually possible in a place like Witherwood. "I heard one of the orderlies telling Orrin that they shot the animal and Archie's okay. Orrin was really happy about it, which is odd. I can't understand why he would care. It seems like he'd rather we were all gone."

Patrick stopped talking to think and sniff.

Meghan took the opportunity to check the watch she was wearing. "The voices will be making the rounds soon. We should get Tobias back to his room."

"I don't want to go back to my room," Tobias insisted. "I want out of here. How did you unlock my door?"

"Meghan's a master with locks," Keith said.

Tobias wasn't happy to hear that. Locks were sort of his thing, and now he had competition.

"She can steal things and pick locks," Keith added. "She'd be a perfect crime robot."

"Stop talking about robots, Keith. We need your help, Tobias," Patrick pleaded. "You've been out. You know it's possible. We know it's horrible here, and we don't want to spend our days waiting until . . . well, until we disappear."

Tobias looked at all three of them. Patrick tall and sniffy, Keith short and with glasses, and Meghan with her uneasy smile and dark eyebrows. They looked like a really useless gang of misfits.

"How did you guys even get here?"

"I lived in Indiana," Meghan said. "I was a foster child, and a social worker offered me the chance to go to an exclusive school. That social worker turned out to be a Catcher. I was glaze-brained for six months before I had it knocked out of me."

"I'm an orphan," Keith said. "I think my parents were professional clowns. They probably died in a really funny but sad way. At least that's what I like to think. I was glaze-brained for about six months too."

"I don't know how I got here," Patrick said. "I've been here as long as I can remember. I used to think this was just what the world is. My brain has been glazed a few times. I've been clear for over four months now. I don't think I've ever been off the top of this mesa."

"Well, let's change that," Tobias said. "I'm pretty happy to have other clearheaded friends. So we really need to keep from being talked at again. Keep your brain clean. We also need to find out what's on the third floor. I think that could help."

"There's only one way we know of to get to the third floor without having to go through the second floor," Patrick said. "We've seen the door. It's in Severe Hall, near the library. There's a set of thin stairs that are hidden behind a large hanging tapestry. The stairs go directly to the third floor."

"All right," Tobias said with enthusiasm. "Tomorrow night we will climb those stairs, but I don't think all of us should go. It'll be too noisy."

"I'm super quiet," Keith said. "I once sat still for almost a whole day."

"You should go with Tobias," Meghan said. "I'll keep an eye on his sister. Patrick's bed is the hardest one to sneak away from, plus the sniffing."

"Good. It'll be me and Keith." Tobias stood up and walked toward the black door.

"We don't leave that way," Patrick said, waving. "That door leads to a far hall that might leave us exposed."

Patrick walked back behind one of the boilers. Against the wall was a large metal panel that kept the hissing boiler from scorching the wall. Patrick grabbed the top right corner and Meghan grabbed the left. They pushed on the corners and a soft clicking noise could be heard. They lowered the sheet of metal like a shade that was being retracted downward.

"Nice," Tobias whispered.

"This school is filled with a lot of openings and secret passages," Patrick said. "And the great thing is, most of the staff doesn't even know they exist. The school was built so long ago that probably only Marvin Withers knows—and Marvin doesn't get around much. We've never seen another person using these passages."

"I've discovered a few passages myself," Tobias said. "It almost makes me like this place. Almost."

All four kids stepped into the wall. Patrick and Meghan then pulled the metal sheet back into place while Keith flipped on a small flashlight.

The space between the walls was thin, but there was more than enough room for them. Patrick led them through the maze of walls and they popped out beneath the stairs not far from Tobias's room.

"You can go the rest of the way by yourself," Patrick whispered. "Tomorrow night, meet Keith right here at eleven thirty."

"I don't have a clock," Tobias said. "And the window in my room is covered in wood. I can't tell if it's morning or night."

"Here." Meghan took off her watch and handed it to Tobias. "It's a gift. Actually, I found it in the lost-and-found box by the cafeteria. I think one of the staff members threw it in there because they couldn't figure out how to set it."

Tobias took the old digital watch and slipped it into his pocket.

"Now," Meghan asked, "do you need me to come to your room and show you how to pick your lock?"

"No, thanks, I can figure it out."

It was a stubborn answer, but Tobias was going to need to be stubborn—and tenacious and cunning—if he was ever going to figure a way out of Witherwood.

"Okay, then, here." Meghan handed Tobias a small black key. "Ms. Gulp had a dozen extras made when she put in a few new locks. She keeps them in the kitchen on a ring. I may have accidentally taken one. It's how I opened your door earlier."

"It's way easier to pick a lock when you have a key," Tobias said.

Meghan smiled, and Tobias kind of liked it.

"Yeah, I'm actually not good at it," she admitted. "But I can find things."

Tobias left his new friends and returned to his room with a much lighter heart. It's interesting to note how hopeful one feels simply by having supporters and a plan.

He locked himself in and took a few moments to write some things down on his hidden papers. He also drew the boiler room they had met in and the new space behind the walls on his big map.

Witherwood was taking shape.

CHAPTER 9

BAG IT

Saying one thing and then doing another can be a real problem. If you promise someone you care about that you'll pick them up next to the crate of dynamite before the wick runs out, you had better be true to your word. Or if you promise the person you love that you'll make sure to pack his or her parachute before you get on a rickety plane, you need to be telling the truth. But if you tell three kids you just met that you're going to go to sleep, and then you sneak out to do some exploring on your own, that's not such a bad thing.

Tobias was just that kind of a "not such a bad kid."

After about an hour, he used the black key Meghan had given him and helped himself out of his room and back into the hall. According to his new watch, it was

one in the morning. Things seemed much calmer. Tobias couldn't hear any screaming or singing voices patrolling the school.

Quietly, he walked down Weary Hall. He passed door number eight, with the carving of the eagle carrying a fish in its talons, and kept going until he reached number nine. On the front of Fiddle's door, there was an eagle with a snake in its claws. Tobias hadn't seen or heard from Fiddle since Fiddle had helped them escape. He was worried that Marvin had punished him. So before checking out the third floor or finding Charlotte, Tobias wanted to look in on Fiddle.

Door number nine was unlocked.

Tobias pushed open the door and slipped inside. The room was completely quiet. He flipped on the lights and the smell of ozone filled the air. Fiddle's bed was still positioned in the middle of the room. The purple curtains that hung around it were open, and it was clear that the bed was empty. In fact, the bed was completely bare—no sheets, no pillows. Tobias looked around the room. It appeared that nobody was living here any longer. Even the dresser drawer that was once filled with pens was now empty. Tobias checked the connecting bathroom. No Fiddle.

"This probably isn't good," Tobias told himself.

Leaving Fiddle's room, he went back to the secret door beneath the stairs. He opened it by pushing the bottom right corner with his toes. He then slipped in and closed it behind him. Instead of heading toward the boiler room, he moved in the opposite direction.

The space behind the walls was tight and dark. He would have loved to have had a flashlight, but once his eyes adjusted he could make out things in the gray well enough to move around. He felt his way down the hall for twenty feet and then came to a fork in the wall space.

Tobias headed right.

He had been behind some of the walls of Witherwood before, but what he really wanted was to find a private stairwell or path that would take him to the other floors. The passage turned two more times. Tobias had brought a pen, and as he walked he slowly drew a line along his arm indicating the turns and spaces he was experiencing. He wanted to make sure he could accurately draw it out when he returned to his room. Two more turns and he came to a set of stairs. It was a bit disappointing, however, because they went down when he wanted them to go up.

Tobias descended the six stairs carefully and walked through a short tunnel with a low celling. He hit another set of six stairs that brought him back up behind a first-floor wall.

"That must have taken me below the main hallway," he said to himself, as if someone was right next to him asking for a report.

He felt his way by touching the wall. When he reached another

fork in the passage, he stopped. To the right, there was darkness. To the left, there was darkness that wasn't quite as dark.

Tobias headed toward the lighter dark.

In the far distance, at the end of the passage, he saw what appeared to be a vent on the wall, about waist-high. The vent was letting in a weak light from outside. Tobias also heard the buzz and rattle of cicadas. He moved quickly, and when he reached the vent, he fell to his knees. He could feel cobwebs on his hands but he couldn't see the thin strands hidden in the dark. He brushed the cobwebs away and looked out the narrow slits of the vent into the courtyard gardens. Warm air wafted in and caused his nose to itch.

He fought back a sneeze, holding it in until it disappeared.

The vent was metal, and there was no give when he tried to push it out. Below the vent, however, there was a wooden peg. Tobias slid the peg six inches to the right, and the vent, as well as a good part of the wall, opened like a small door into the courtyard. He pushed and stepped out with his right foot. Looking through some bushes, he could see that he was in the gardens near the end of Severe Hall. The temptation to explore further was strong, but the fear of what was out there was stronger. Tobias backed in, closed the wall, and slid the wooden peg into place. As he turned to head back down the passage, he heard some people in the garden talking.

"Enough," a gravelly voice said.

Tobias froze. He pushed his left ear and eye up to the vent and tried to see where the speaking was coming from.

"It's time for you to come with me," the same voice said.

"Can I just go to sleep?" another voice asked. "I think I'm tired."

Tobias's heart raced. He didn't recognize the first voice, but he knew the second one.

"Archie," Tobias whispered.

"Come with me," the gravelly voice ordered. "You'll get plenty of sleep where you're going."

"Thanks," Archie said.

The conversation was too far away for Tobias to see who was bossing Archie around. Concerned for his friend, he slid the wooden peg once more and quietly pushed the wall open. Tobias crawled out of the opening, keeping his body close to the ground and remaining hidden behind the bushes. He was worried about animals attacking him, but his desire to help Archie was stronger than his fear.

"Be what you were born to be," the voice told Archie. "Follow me, and sleep will never be a concern again."

Tobias crawled beneath a bush to the right of him. From under the wide leaves, he could now see Archie. His shirt looked torn, and he wore no shoes, but he appeared to be okay. His head glowed under the light of one of the lamps lining a stone path. It was a relief to know he was alive. It was a horror to see who was talking to him.

Marvin, Tobias gasped.

Marvin Withers, a direct descendant of Hyrum Withers, the founder of Witherwood, was a horrible person. He was currently sitting in a small electric wagon near Archie. Tobias couldn't see Marvin's repulsive face because he was wearing a thin bag over it with a hat on top of the bag. Marvin's voice was so smooth when he spoke in the square room, but out in the open, it seemed to lack the brain-glazing effect. Like always, there was a feathery ball on Marvin's left shoulder, making him seem like an ugly pirate with a bizarre parrot. The large bird reminded Tobias of Lars and how much Charlotte had liked the little creature. Now his sister was somewhere he didn't know, and he was having to stare at Marvin Withers alone from beneath a bush and watch the old man as he sat hunched over in his electric wagon shaking his cane at Archie.

"We saved you for a purpose," Marvin said. "Now follow me."

Marvin pushed a button on the handlebar of the wagon. A soft whining sound started and the little cart moved forward at a slow pace. Archie shuffled after it like a loyal dog.

Tobias came out from beneath the bush and slipped across the stone path. He pressed his back up against a large tree, keeping

an eye on Marvin and Archie as they moved farther away and toward the center of the gardens.

The dark night was suspiciously void of other creatures or noises besides the whir of Marvin's cart and the low buzzing of cicadas. There were small glowing rocks all over the ground, reminding Tobias of when he had first arrived at Witherwood.

"This is crazy," Tobias whispered to himself.

"I know," Keith whispered from right beside him.

Tobias's heart leapt up his throat and almost burst from his mouth. Keith was standing behind him.

Tobias caught his breath and hit Keith lightly on the shoulder. "You nearly scared me to death."

"I told you I was quiet." Keith's prickly hair made his silhouette look cartoonish.

Tobias sniffed. "Are you wearing hair gel?"

"Maybe," Keith said. "Meghan gave me some she found."

"That's why I didn't smell you. You smell like a flower."

"Thank you," Keith said sincerely.

"What are you doing here?"

"I was in the space behind the wall when I heard someone pass. I followed the noise and found you looking out of that vent. I was going to say something, but I wanted to see what you were up to."

"Archie's out here," Tobias said. "He's with Marvin."

"And you think it's a good idea to follow them?"

"If I can help Archie, I'm going to."

"What if you get caught?" Keith asked, pushing up his glasses with his thumb. "You'll be no help to your sister, or us, if you're captured."

"I'm not letting Archie go with that lunatic," Tobias said. "So you can come with me or stay here."

"Come with you of course," Keith said almost happily.

They had to move quickly. Their short conversation had given Marvin and Archie a nice lead. Tobias found trees and stones to easily hide behind as they carefully followed the whir of the cart. True to his word, Keith was very quiet. Tobias had to keep checking to see if he was still following.

"I told you," Keith whispered as Tobias looked back. "I'm super stealthy."

They were at the center of the gardens. Even in the dark, Tobias could see a faint outline of the square building.

Keith slipped up right behind him. "What do we do if they go inside? We can't follow them in there."

Tobias ignored Keith and quietly darted across the path and back behind a thick stretch of bushes that smelled sweet but were covered with sticky thorns.

"Seriously," Keith insisted, so close Tobias could feel his breath. "We can't go in there. You know what happens inside. Marvin starts talking and everyone's mind turns to poop."

Tobias turned to Keith.

"Sorry, I meant mess."

"I know what you meant," Tobias said with a smile. "I just forgot that you're the funny one."

"Hey, what's he doing?" Keith whispered with excitement.

Tobias looked through the thorny bush. Marvin was up ahead on his wagon, and Archie was right behind him. They had turned off the path and Marvin was motoring toward a huge boulder with a tree standing near it. He stopped in front of the tree.

"See that hole?" Marvin asked Archie while pointing with his cane.

Archie turned his head and focused on a small black hole in the tree trunk.

"Stick your hand in there," Marvin ordered. "Reach up and pull down on the small chain. I'd do it myself, but my hands don't have that kind of strength these days."

Archie stepped right up to the tree. He put his hand in the dark hole and rooted around like it was a piñata with a single piece of candy lost inside it.

"I think I found it," Archie said.

"Then pull."

Archie's arm tightened and he yanked the chain. A hissing noise rose from the soil like steam. The large boulder near Marvin shook and then rolled backward, exposing a hole in the ground where a small path could be seen. The round feathery ball on Marvin's shoulder shook and snorted.

"There, there, Capricious," Marvin said, petting his bird. "We will find you food soon. Now, come with us, boy."

Archie followed Marvin as he drove his electric wagon down into the hole. In less than thirty seconds they were all gone, and the stone was rolling back into place.

"Unbelievable," Tobias whispered.

"I know," Keith said with disgust. "Who names a pet Capricious? I like pet names like Steven or Gary. Aren't capriciouses some kind of pants?"

"I'm not talking about Marvin's pet. I'm talking about where they disappeared to."

"Oh, well, we can't go in there," Keith said, being the voice of reason instead of the funny one for a moment. "We should get back to our beds. We'll regroup tomorrow and let Patrick and Meghan know what's going on. If we get taken now, nobody will even know what happened to us."

"That's true," Tobias agreed. "So you go back, and if I don't make it out alive, tell them what happened."

"Awwww," Keith whined. "You know I won't leave. I'm way too curious and not smart enough to make the right choice for myself."

"Then we're going in."

"I can't think of a single funny thing to say about that."

"I can't either," Tobias admitted.

The two boys crept out from behind the bush and over to the tree with the dark hole.

"We should wait a few minutes," Keith suggested. "Just in case they are still near and can hear the rock opening."

It was a good suggestion, so they both stood there until Tobias's patience ran out. He thrust his arm into the hole, located the chain, and pulled. The large bolder popped and crackled and then rolled back, exposing the entrance in the ground.

They stared down into the wide hole. There was a smooth stone ramp leading to a concrete path. The opening was circled by small glowing stones.

"Ready?" Tobias asked.

"Nope."

Tobias moved into the hole anyway.

CHAPTER 10

THE UNDERGROUND POOL

Most people have five senses—seeing, hearing, touching, tasting, and smelling. I know a man who sells hats who claims to have a sixth sense he calls fitting. He has the ability to guess anyone's hat size. Now, whether or not he really does have some superhero fitting power, it doesn't change the fact that there are at least five senses.

Tobias could see the path that led down below the rolling stone. He could hear the quiet and knew that Marvin's wagon was nowhere near. He could touch the walls of the tunnel and feel the cool wet surface. He couldn't taste anything, which was sad because he was hungry, but he could smell something delicious, like cinnamon rolls being pulled from the oven. The smell made his hungry stomach even more so.

"Do you smell that?" Keith asked quietly.

It was a silly question; Tobias smelled almost everything.

"Does this lead to some sort of top secret underground bakery? I hope so," Keith said, answering his own question.

The concrete path was narrow. After the initial slope, it had leveled out and the tunnel was twisting in a horseshoe pattern, turning them in the other direction. There were tiny lights on the tunnel walls every dozen steps. The bulbs were as small as mushrooms, but they lit things up enough to easily see the way.

"Seriously," Keith said. "That's the best smell I've ever smelled. And I've smelled some pretty amazing things in my life."

"Really?"

"Yeah, I once smelled a chocolate orange."

"That's amazing," Tobias said sarcastically.

"What? You don't think a chocolate orange would smell good?"

"Shhhh," Tobias whispered.

The tunnel looped again, and they could hear Marvin's voice. The two of them pressed their backs to the wall and inched closer. As the path turned, it opened up to a large white room lit with bright white bulbs. Two big planted ferns near the boys made the perfect spot to hide and witness what was happening.

They slipped behind the ferns.

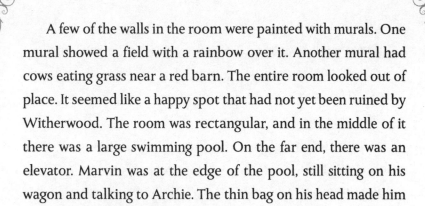

A few of the walls in the room were painted with murals. One mural showed a field with a rainbow over it. Another mural had cows eating grass near a red barn. The entire room looked out of place. It seemed like a happy spot that had not yet been ruined by Witherwood. The room was rectangular, and in the middle of it there was a large swimming pool. On the far end, there was an elevator. Marvin was at the edge of the pool, still sitting on his wagon and talking to Archie. The thin bag on his head made him even more sinister-looking.

"We are quite happy that the Protector didn't kill you when it carried you off," Marvin said. "You're valuable—worth much more to us alive than dead."

"Thanks," Archie said, standing next to Marvin and staring down into the pool. "What's that down there?"

Archie pointed toward the water.

"You should know better than to ask questions," Marvin chided. His voice was stern now, and he sounded like an adult who wanted everyone to know he was serious.

"Sorry about the question," Archie apologized.

"Don't worry," Marvin cooed. "This is the moment. The water looks inviting, doesn't it?"

Archie nodded enthusiastically.

"Take a dip. I believe you're ready for it."

Tobias was stumped. Archie seemed fine, and the only thing

that Marvin was doing was offering him a chance to go swimming—
something most kids wanted to do—something Tobias himself
wouldn't have minded doing.

"Do we stop him?" Keith whispered.

"I'm not sure."

Archie took off his shirt, and after waiting no more than half
a second, he dove into the water. There was a tremendous splash
and Marvin laughed as if he were a kindly old grandfather who
was enjoying the happiness his grandchild was experiencing.

"Swim around," Marvin said. "Take your time. You've earned it."

Archie splashed happily as he swam back and forth.

"Are we trying to save Archie from having fun?" Keith
whispered.

"I don't know what's happening," Tobias admitted. "I never
expected to find a cinnamon-roll-smelling swimming pool. I'm
really confused."

"It's weird, but we should get back," Keith said. "If we leave
now, we might have a chance to slip into our rooms without being
noticed. Of course, if the punishment is getting to spend time in a
swimming pool, I'm not sure I don't want to get caught."

Tobias began to inch away from the tall potted ferns and back
into the tunnel. As soon as they were far enough, they picked up
their pace and ran all the way to the rolling rock.

"What time is it?" Keith asked as they ran.

"It's two thirty."

"That's the best time to go to the dentist," Keith said. "Get it? Tooth hurty."

"That's not funny."

They made it out of the hole and Tobias pulled the chain in the tree and closed the rolling stone. The garden wasn't as still as it had been when they went into the tunnel. Tobias could see a few pairs of eyes reflecting off the light from a nearby lamppost and hear leaves rustling.

"I think we should run."

They ran through the bushes and trees and met up with the bit of wall that opened. Both of them slipped inside the wall, and Tobias shut the vent and slid the wooden peg back into place.

"That was really weird, right?" Tobias asked.

"Very," Keith said. "But it smelled good. Now I'm hungry."

"I just hope Archie's okay."

"Are any of us really okay?" Keith asked.

It was a very good point.

"Can you make it back to your room?"

"Of course," Tobias said, sounding slightly insulted.

"Sorry, I forgot you probably know your way around this place as well as me. So we'll meet up beneath the stairs near your room tomorrow night at eleven thirty. Until then, act dumb."

"I will," Tobias said.

The two of them split off where the space forked.

Tobias quickly worked his way back to his room. When he got to his door, he unlocked it with the black key and slipped inside. He flipped on the lights and turned around to discover he was not alone.

"Hello, Tobias."

CHAPTER 11

OCD

Tobias blinked and rubbed his eyes. He looked at the visitor sitting on his cot and rubbed his eyes some more. "Fiddle."

Tobias didn't know whether he should hug his friend or keep away. It was nearly impossible to tell who could be trusted at Witherwood. Also, it wasn't like Fiddle ever showered.

Fiddle stood up. His long dark hair was still long and stringy, and it hung in his face like wet noodles. He had on a white T-shirt and black jeans. His eyes jumped and darted as he studied Tobias.

"You look different," Fiddle said.

"I'm the same person," Tobias replied.

"I can see that; you just look different. Maybe it's because you're not standing in a cement tunnel with your sister, trying to escape."

"That could be it," Tobias said, smiling. "That was the last place you saw me."

"Where's your sister?"

"She's been moved to a different room."

"Oh. I used to think you two were just my imagination. But my uncle told me you aren't. He also said I should stay far away from you."

"So why are you here, then?"

"Sometimes my uncle's a jerk," Fiddle said, tapping his pointer finger against his leg as he spoke. "He's also really hard to look at. Don't tell anyone, but sometimes I'm embarrassed to be related."

"I won't tell anyone."

Fiddle looked around the room. "I think this is the first time I've been behind door number seven. It's not that great."

"I agree."

"So what happened?" Fiddle asked. "I thought you and your sister were leaving."

Tobias sat down on the cot Charlotte had last used.

"Oh, this is a sit-down conversation," Fiddle said seriously, sitting back down on another cot.

"We got caught," Tobias said. "Sheriff Pidge brought us back."

"He's a horse's behind," Fiddle said. "Although he usually gives me gum."

"You know him?"

"I get to know everyone who comes around here," Fiddle said. "Remember, Marvin's my uncle."

"So what's your story?" Tobias asked.

"I wasn't breathing when I was born. I guess the lack of oxygen left me a little touched in the head."

"No," Tobias said. "What happened to you after we left you in the tunnel?"

"Right. Well, I held on to the hatch, keeping it closed as long as I could. Once the Protector left, I stepped out into the stream. There were a bunch of orderlies waiting for me there. They were pretty mad that you guys got away. They brought me back to my room. That's when I gave you my pillows. Then my uncle decided to put me in a different room where I wouldn't be so alone. He also told me what a big disappointment I am and how I'll never be anything but an embarrassment to my family name."

Fiddle stopped talking to breathe deeply.

"I'm sorry," Tobias said. "We shouldn't have asked you to help us. Thank you for doing what you did for us."

"I'm glad I did. It was the most fun I've had in a while. I wish that girl was here."

"Charlotte?"

"Yeah, she was interesting. Remember how she kept saying I couldn't get you off the mesa?"

"I do."

"She was wrong."

"That's true. We might have gotten caught, but we did get off the mesa. Where's your room now?"

"I don't really remember," Fiddle admitted. "Down some hall, up another. There's always music playing. I can't stand it. It's kind of small, and I'd been in my old room so long that now I feel lost."

"Sorry."

"I'm supposed to stay put, but once I step out of my room, it takes me a while to find my way back. Usually that angry rat lady has to point me in the right direction."

"Well, I'm glad you're all right."

"That's funny. Why would someone be glad about that?" Fiddle asked.

"Um, because we're friends."

"Interesting," Fiddle said seriously. "That's a first. So do you still want to get out of Witherwood?"

"Yes, but not without my sister."

"It must be nice to have someone you care about. Can I tell you something?"

Tobias nodded.

"They locked up that hatch we entered in the stream last time. So if you do get out, don't try to go that way. Also the Protectors are out of control."

"I've noticed."

"My uncle plans to kill them all," Fiddle said. "They are the results of some bad experiments and they used to protect the school. Now things are different. My uncle wants all of them dead. I guess one of them almost accidentally lit the barn on fire while tearing things up behind the school. That barn would have burned for hours, and he says he can't have that. So my uncle is calling in some people to take care of it."

"What people?"

"I don't know, but if you're wandering around outside, I'd be careful. I'd hate to see you get hurt or shot."

"Thanks."

Fiddle stood up. "Well, I should try to find my way back. Will you tell Charlotte I was right?"

"The moment I see her again."

"There was something else," Fiddle said, thinking. "Something important. Oh yeah, I heard my uncle tell Orrin that they were expecting all new students this next semester."

"Really? So Witherwood will be super crowded?"

"No," Fiddle said in a friendly tone. "He said all the old ones will be gone."

Tobias didn't move. The words had taken his breath away. He tried to blink but his mind was too busy processing what Fiddle had said.

"Well, have a good sleep." Fiddle patted Tobias on the shoulder as he walked past him. He slipped out the door and into the hall.

"Wait," Tobias whispered.

Fiddle stuck his head back in.

"What's happening to us, the old students?"

"I'm not sure, but I think it's bad."

"This isn't good."

"Right," Fiddle said, confused. "That's why I said it was bad."

"This is probably more important than you telling me the hatch was locked up."

"I know," Fiddle said apologetically. "I never know if I should give people the bad news or the worst news first."

CHAPTER 12

GARAGE SALE

Ralph Eggers was not the kind of person they would ever put on the front of a coin or a postage stamp. Not that he wasn't kindhearted or deserving in some way, but he just wasn't a success. I suppose if they designed a coin to honor people who were unlucky in life, Ralph might have a shot at making it onto the halfpenny. Maybe. Even before he lost his memory, he had lost dozens of jobs and ruined many opportunities. Now he had no car or home or family that he knew of. Hope was a hard thing for him to find. He wanted to be the kind of person who found possibility in everything, but he was more like the kind of person who would possibly mess up everything. His life was a mess of nothing: no job, no family, no memories.

Ralph closed his eyes and tried to remember anything.

"Are you asleep?" Sam asked. "I know it's early, but you're not going to recognize anything with your eyes closed."

"I know," Ralph answered. "I don't think I'm ever going to figure stuff out. My mind's blank, and it feels like it might always be that way."

It was early morning, and Sam and Ralph were driving along the outskirts of town trying to see if any landmark or landscape might trigger Ralph's memory. They had been driving through neighborhoods and parks and downtown for the last two days, just hoping something would seem familiar.

"Don't lose hope," Sam urged. "It's best not to give up until you're beat."

"I think I'm beat."

"Not completely. You got one of the finest drivers in the world personally toting you around. We haven't covered the whole city, so we can't quit yet. I know this city better than anyone," Sam bragged. "I mean, that makes sense, seeing as how I'm a taxi driver. I take great pride in knowing where to go."

"You must be very proud."

"Thank you. I've met other drivers who just follow maps and GPS coordinates. That ain't driving. It's cheating."

"You're right."

"Ahh, you're probably just agreeing with me. But that's okay. It makes sense that you would agree, seeing as how I'm right."

"I don't want to be ungrateful," Ralph said. "But it seems to me that you aren't making any money by driving me around all day."

"I've got savings," Sam boasted. "I want to see this through. Plus, I feel a little sorry for you. No offense."

"None taken."

"I mean, I'm my own man. That's why I do this job. If I wanna tell the world to go take a flying leap, I can. It's a comforting feeling."

"Well, I'll never be able to thank you enough."

"That's probably true. Just remember me one day when you discover you're a rich king or billionaire business guy and give me a good tip."

"For sure."

As they drove around, nothing triggered Ralph's memories. Everything just looked like houses in a city that had no connection to him whatsoever. Before lunch, Sam pulled over at a garage sale.

"Mind if I rummage through things a bit? I like garage sales. I once bought a lamp for a couple of bucks and found out later it was worth three thousand dollars."

Ralph couldn't argue with that.

The two men got out and walked up to the driveway. There

was junk lying everywhere. Old mattresses, workout equipment, books, tools, records, etc. . . . Sam went directly for the lamps.

The house that the garage belonged to was weathered and old, with a Victorian roofline and gold-painted rain gutters. There was a big porch, and the front yard was covered in deep-green grass. Ralph didn't really need anything, but he wanted to make sure Sam didn't feel rushed. So he flipped through the records and tried the exercise bike in an effort to look interested.

There was a lot of junk for sale. There were also a few other people milling around, all of them with stuff in their arms. Near the garage door, there was a man wearing a floral shirt and black shorts. He had a poorly grown beard and a baseball cap with a tiger on the front. The man was sitting on a lawn chair next to a metal box that was filled with money.

"See anything you like?" the man asked Ralph as he looked at a ceramic vase.

"Not yet," Ralph said kindly. "There's a lot of stuff. Are you moving?"

"No," the man said casually. "I do this for a living. I collect stuff from other antique shops, garage sales, estate sales, you name it. Then I bring it home, mark it up a little, and sell it. I'm not the richest guy around, but I've been to Hawaii on vacation, and I have a boat."

"Wow."

"Wanna see it? I've got it back behind the house."

"That's okay."

"It's a thirty-footer."

"Neat," Ralph said, still looking at vases.

"That's entirely not true. It's actually a twenty-footer. But that's still a real boat. I don't care what the local boating chapter says. It's seaworthy."

"Great."

"And I bought it all with the money from my garage sales." The man took a long drink from the big cup he was holding. "So, are you gonna buy one of those vases or just look at them?"

"I'm only looking. My friend might buy."

"Just so you know, I've got a Ping-Pong table inside the house that's for sale. It doesn't have a super-level surface, but it still plays okay. Interested?"

"Nope," Ralph said, moving farther away.

Having seen his fill of ceramic vases, he moved to a table filled with picture frames for sale. Some of the frames were empty, while others had old photos in them. Ralph had no need for a frame, as he had no pictures or memories to put on display. But as he stepped past them, something caught his eye. He glanced down and locked in on a brown frame with a single pink flower painted on the top of it. The frame was unremarkable, but the picture was quite the opposite.

"Remarkable," Ralph remarked.

He picked up the frame and turned around quickly.

"Sam!"

Sam was elbow-deep in a box of old salt- and pepper shakers. He looked up like a prairie dog and spotted Ralph and his ghost-white face. With no more than five giant steps, Sam was standing next to Ralph, asking him if he was okay.

"I think so," Ralph said excitedly. "Look at this."

Sam took the frame from Ralph and studied it. It was a picture of two children. One was a boy about twelve years old and the other was a girl about a year younger. They were standing in a field by themselves.

"Do you know these kids?" Sam asked.

"They were at that school on that mesa. Remember?"

"I didn't go into the building with you," Sam said apologetically. "These are those crazy swearing kids you saw?"

"I think so," Ralph said breathlessly. "This has to mean something, right?"

"Let's find out."

Sam took the picture up to the man with the floral shirt and the twenty-foot boat. Ralph followed right behind.

"Excuse me, do you know these kids?" Sam asked, thrusting the picture forward.

The man took the photo and frame and glanced at them. "No idea. That's just a frame I picked up somewhere."

"Where?" Ralph said desperately. "Where did you pick it up? Was it here in town? Some other city? This could be really important."

"Like I was telling you earlier, I go to a lot of garage sales and flea markets and auctions. I'm in this full-time. I've got a boat."

"Yeah, yeah, you told me that," Ralph said impatiently. "But look at it really hard and think. If you're the professional that you say you are, you should be able to recall where you picked it up."

The man studied the picture like it was a puzzle written in a language he didn't understand. He turned it upside down and looked at it that way.

"It may have been in a box of stuff I bought yesterday from a woman," he said with some confidence.

"A woman?" Ralph asked excitedly. "Do you know her name?"

"She wasn't a real pleasant woman. I think her name was Margaret."

"Or Martha?"

"Could have been."

Ralph was beside himself.

Sam was beside Ralph and whispered, "Unbelievable."

"Whoever she was, she sold me a box of things she said she needed to get rid of."

"What other things were in the box?" Ralph asked.

"I can't remember. I bought a lot of things from a few different places yesterday. But whatever I bought must be scattered around here, or I might have sold them."

"You should look around," Sam said to Ralph. "See if anything else hits you."

"Wait," the bearded boat man said. He flipped the picture frame over and bent the tabs holding the back on. He removed the felt easel and pulled out the rectangular piece of cardboard. Ralph and Sam leaned in, looking at the frame as if it were a candy bar that held the last golden ticket. On the back of the photo Ralph could see three words:

Tobias and Charlotte.

CHAPTER 13

THE THIRD FLOOR

Guessing is a good way to get yourself into trouble. Go ahead, guess what's behind that door, over that hill, beneath that murky water. Wrong. There is a net behind that door, a shack over that hill, and a sunken boat beneath that murky water. Guess what they're all for. Sorry, wrong again. The net's to hold you still, the shack's to hold you captive, and the boat beneath the murky water? Two words: watery grave. See? Guessing can lead to some uncomfortable spots.

Tobias was tired of guessing what his future was going to hold. He was a child of action. He made a quick list of all the things he needed to take care of. He wrote down things like: Find Charlotte. Search the library for information about

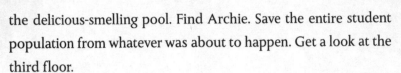

the delicious-smelling pool. Find Archie. Save the entire student population from whatever was about to happen. Get a look at the third floor.

It was not going to be an easy list to complete, but Tobias felt like he should start with the end in mind. Or start at the end of the list.

Find out what's on the third floor.

He slept for a few moments and then lay on his cot, wishing the pain in his stomach over the hunger he had and the worry he felt would go away. He also wished the swollen black eye that Meghan had given him would stop hurting.

At exactly six in the morning, Ms. Gulp tromped through his door and began barking orders.

"Get up. Get ready. Get."

As Tobias stood up, she noticed his black eye. She reached out and grabbed his chin to look more closely.

"What happened to you?"

"I fell out of bed," Tobias said slowly, trying to sound as dim-witted as he could.

"What a slow child," Ms. Gulp said, *tsking*. "Can't even sleep right."

Tobias thanked her for her comments and then walked to the bathroom and washed up. Cleaned and ready, he followed his boxy taskmaster to the kitchen. It took a lot of focus to look simple and thoughtless. Tobias wanted to make sure everyone believed he was still as brainwashed as he was supposed to be.

In the kitchen, there was no sign of Charlotte. Now the tasks they usually did together he was forced to do himself.

While carrying food down to the kitchen cellar, Tobias noticed that there was a much larger lock on the cellar door than before. It looked like the kind of lock one might secure an entire army with. It would take more than bolt cutters to escape through the cellar again.

Students made their way into the cathedral-looking cafeteria and ate their breakfasts while Tobias was kept in the kitchen like always. He tried to listen for his sister, but he never heard her voice. After the breakfast dishes were done, he was escorted to his classes by Orrin.

Orrin's four hairs were sticking straight up and the armpits of his white lab coat were yellow from sweat. His two-colored eyes looked swollen, and the point of his chin quivered as if under pressure.

"Things are a bit uneasy at the moment," Orrin said, as if Tobias needed an explanation. "Better than yesterday, but uneasy. The Protectors are—well . . . things are a bit uneasy. What happened to your face?"

"I fell out of bed."

"What an odd child. Don't let it happen again."

"I won't."

"You can't actually guarantee that," Orrin pointed out. "So why say such a thing? Life is a series of unending problems and there is no certainty that tomorrow will bring anything other than misery, pain, and occasional accidents. Don't you agree?"

Tobias nodded.

"Of course now, thanks to Witherwood, you will help provide happiness to a number of wealthy, I mean, deserving clients. Yes, their lives will be much better off, thanks to your sorry one. I guess it's true what they say: children really are the future."

It wasn't easy for Tobias to suppress the chill running up his spine. He wanted to shake and shiver, but he couldn't give himself away. Orrin wasn't the easiest person to be around. He was even less appealing when he was saying such awful things.

"Regardless of all that," Orrin said as they reached Tobias's classroom, "just remember, don't think about things that shouldn't be thought about."

Tobias just nodded.

In class, Professor Himzakity looked almost as tired and out of sorts as Orrin. Clearly, the staff at Witherwood had been struggling to keep things in order. Himzakity's lecture made even less sense than usual.

"You students need to understand how hard we work to

reform you. . . . Don't forget how many sacrifices we make. . . . Next time you're lying safely in your bed, remember you would be nothing without us."

As instructed, Tobias took notes. He could see Charlotte at the front of the class also taking notes. There was no sign of Archie, and the desk he usually sat in was empty.

I hope he's doing something fun like swimming, Tobias thought.

Patrick and Keith were sitting a couple of desks behind Charlotte. Tobias had never really noticed them before. Meghan was sitting one desk to the right of his sister. It's very possible he might have previously noticed her.

"There are frightening things that you children know nothing about," Professor Himzakity lectured. "You are unaware of all that hides before your eyes. But this is a reform school, so let's hope that changes."

At lunchtime, some women wheeled in carts filled with food. The staff at Witherwood was a curiosity to Tobias. There were lots of orderlies in yellow lab coats and women in blue skirts and brown shirts. All of them looked so similar and none of them really stood out. They seemed more like pillars and lamps than people—fixtures in a school where any rational person would never want to work.

The students tore into the food, trying to make up for all they had missed the day before. Tobias wanted to ask Professor

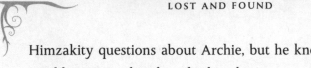

Himzakity questions about Archie, but he knew any curiosity would give away his clear-thinking brain.

As the food was being devoured, a commotion of some sort was brewing outside the classroom windows. Everyone stopped eating to point and stare. Some children stood and walked to the windows. In the courtyard, three burly orderlies were carrying a large feathered beast into the gardens. The animal was strapped to a thick wooden pole, which was resting on the orderlies' shoulders. The creature's head bounced as they walked, making it obvious that whatever it was was no longer alive.

Tobias tried not to act too excited, but he knew he had seen a creature like that before. The thing that had attacked him and Charlotte behind the school and by the stream had looked an awful lot like that dead beast.

Keith slipped into the desk next to Tobias and with a slacked jaw whispered, "I hope there's not too many more of those."

"Me too," Tobias whispered back.

"Children," Professor Himzakity ordered, "away from the windows. Keep your eyes where they should be, on your food. That may look like a dead Protector, but what you just saw is simply a prop that the school will be using for an upcoming play."

Most of the brainwashed students clapped. Tobias joined in so as to appear equally stupid.

"Just eat your food," Himzakity said with disgust.

As all the students moved away from the window and back into seats, Tobias got up and worked his way closer to Charlotte. She looked at him, blinked a couple of times, and continued eating.

"Charlotte," he mouthed.

He winked and tried to get a rise out of her, but she just kept eating as if he were someone she'd never met. It made Tobias sick. His sister was so far gone. She had no control of her thoughts and no way to fend for herself if something bad did go down.

Tobias offered Charlotte part of his sandwich.

"Thanks," she said.

"I love it here," Tobias forced himself to say.

"Me too," she replied.

Sadly, Charlotte needed someone to drop something heavy on her toes a few times. Tobias would have done it, but now was not the right time.

After lunch, Himzakity went on and on about nothing—literally.

"If you think about it, we are all nothing," he lectured. "But especially children. They are extra nothing."

The day dragged, and Tobias could think of little besides his conversation with Fiddle and his need to visit the third floor. He was having a difficult time waiting.

Following class, Tobias was instructed to help in the kitchen for dinner and then clean up after everyone else finished. Once he was done with all the work, he sat at one of the empty tables and ate a cold meal of fried chicken and coleslaw and, of course, pudding.

Tobias's hands were raw from doing so many dishes, and his feet hurt from standing. So it felt good to sit down and finally eat. He polished off the chicken and coleslaw and dove into the pudding. It was delicious, as usual. It was also a constant at Witherwood. No meal was ever served without pudding. If Witherwood wasn't such a horrible place, they could have manufactured the stuff and sold it worldwide. It was *that* good. It didn't taste like any other pudding Tobias had ever eaten. It really was the one thing he looked forward to in the day. He would have some at breakfast. There was always some at lunch. And dinner seemed to be pudding-heavy as well.

Tobias stopped eating his pudding and breathed in deep. He set his spoon down and looked at the half-eaten bowl of the chocolaty treat—with horror.

"There's something in the pudding," he whispered.

Tobias took another sniff. He couldn't identify the smell and he couldn't believe he had been so stupid. He wanted to simultaneously throw up and cry. He wanted to throw up to get rid of the pudding he had swallowed, and he wanted to cry because now he couldn't have more.

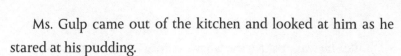

Ms. Gulp came out of the kitchen and looked at him as he stared at his pudding.

"Eat your pudding. Then I'll escort you to your room."

It all made sense. There was something in the pudding. The pudding was delivered in big cans through the kitchen cellar. Then Ms. Gulp would open the cans and pour the stuff into a big bowl where she would mix it until, as she said . . .

"It's smooth and ready."

Ms. Gulp walked off and Tobias pushed his food away.

Ready for what?

He picked up his tray and cleaned his spot, already wishing he could eat some more pudding. He was taken to his room by a huffing and moaning Ms. Gulp. She was the sort of person who was always out of sorts, but today she was completely unsorted.

"I don't know why I have to do such menial things," she complained. "Walking a child to his room is beneath me. Children should be obscene not heard."

"You're right," Tobias said, making sure to sound dumb but secretly wishing he could correct what she had just said.

Ms. Gulp allowed Tobias to use the restroom and then she locked him up in his space. Before walking off, she yelled through the door.

"You're lucky you're locked in. There are children in Africa who would love such a privilege."

"Thanks!" Tobias yelled.

Once he was positive she wasn't coming back, Tobias took out his papers from beneath the floorboard and wrote down a few more important details. The most important being...

There's something about the pudding! Don't eat it!

He pulled out the watch Meghan had lent him and noticed the time.

8:27 p.m.

Tobias was exhausted and there were still three hours before he was supposed to meet Keith. So, he lay down on his bed for just a second.

Many seconds later he was awakened by Keith standing over him and tapping him on his right shoulder. Waking up to Keith and his large glasses can give a person quite a start.

"How'd you get in here?" Tobias asked. "You startled me."

"Meghan got me a key too."

"I guess that's okay," Tobias said, sitting up. "What time is it?"

"It's almost midnight. I waited in the passageway, but you never came."

"I guess I fell asleep."

"I think that's a pretty good guess," Keith said, pushing his glasses up. "You were snoring like a sleep robot. Are you ready?"

Tobias was so tired, but he practically jumped off his cot—it was finally time to visit the third floor. They left his room and crossed the hall. Tobias led Keith to the lockers at the far end of Weary Hall.

"I found this passage last week," Tobias whispered. "Right before my sister and I escaped."

"Just think," Keith whispered back, "if you had gotten away, we wouldn't be here right now."

"And that's a bad thing?"

"For me it would be."

Tobias popped open the locker and they both stepped in. Keith had brought his flashlight, which made moving around through the walls much less dangerous. In no time at all, they were behind of the bookshelves in the library. Tobias slid the low shelf open and the two of them crawled out.

The library was dead.

Not a single light was on, and the dark sky outside the windows was refusing to share even a pinprick of starlight.

"I don't think Patrick knows about that passage," Keith whispered.

"I figured it would get us here quickest."

Keith swept his flashlight around the deserted library. Books and boxes still sat just where they had been sitting before. The circular counter in the middle of the room looked like a mouth that was permanently stuck saying the letter O.

"It's weird," Keith said. "I used to hate to read, but I think

I would love a book now. There's never anything to do besides lie on my bed and stare at the ceiling. I guess that's fine for those who still have goopy brains, but I can't take it much longer. It seems like a book would be amazing. I'm pretty tired of my own thoughts."

"I don't think anyone would notice if you took a book."

Keith grabbed two small books and slipped them into his back pockets. "I don't even care what they're about."

They walked around the bookcases and past the counter. At the library entrance, Tobias unlocked the door and they both stepped into the hall. They took a turn to the left and they were now standing in front of a large hanging tapestry. The ceiling in this hall was at least twenty feet tall, and the tapestry ran from the top of the wall to the bottom. There was gold rope outlining the entire tapestry, and a massive picture of a goat with a crown on its head was stitched on the front.

"The stairs are behind there," Keith said.

Tobias reached out and grabbed an edge. He tried to pull the tapestry away from the wall but it was stuck to it.

"Here," Keith said, handing Tobias the flashlight. "You have to roll it up from the bottom."

Keith leaned down and grabbed the very bottom edge. With some effort, he rolled the center part of the tapestry up twelve inches. It wasn't easy to see, but the pattern on the material

disguised what was a nice-sized flap that Keith was now pushing up. Tobias saw steps hidden behind the material. He would have been excited about it, but down the hall they could hear singing voices patrolling the school.

"Someone's coming," Tobias warned. He flipped the flashlight off. "Roll faster."

Keith pushed up the fabric as fast as he could. The singing voices were getting closer and there was a soft gray beam of light at the end of the hall. Tobias reached down and pulled the cloth up a couple more inches. Keith crawled through the opening. Tobias didn't have to be told to follow. He crawled back behind the tapestry and let the flap drop, closing them in on the thin stairs hidden behind it. Neither one moved a muscle as the sound of someone softly singing grew nearer and nearer.

Footsteps passed in front of the tapestry while the song drifted through the material and rested on their ears.

> *The way is clear; the means are mighty*
> *In glow of day or on the night sea.*
> *Repent, repair, and wish them well.*
> *Too soon to tell, too soon to tell.*

The footsteps faded and soon the sound of singing was no longer audible.

"There's nothing funny about that," Keith said.

"Yeah, a little too close for comfort. Come on."

Tobias turned and began to climb the stairs. "Who found these stairs anyway?"

"Andy. He found all the passages we know of."

"Do you think he actually made it out?" Tobias asked.

"I do, but he was kind of a jerk. I know Meghan likes him and all, but he wasn't a nice person. He probably made it out and just didn't bother to tell anyone or find a way to rescue us."

"I don't think anyone would do that," Tobias said. "If I ever get out, I'm telling the whole world about this awful place."

"I feel the same way, but I have to admit that some days I wonder why I want to get out," Keith confessed. "I mean there's bad stuff happening here, but I'm not sure what I have to go home to isn't worse."

"Sometimes I think the same thing," Tobias admitted. "I'll get out and my dad will bring me right back. But now I need to be away from this place. It's all about getting out."

"That's a good saying," Keith said. "I can picture that on a bumper sticker."

Both boys became quiet as they climbed. At the top of the stairs there was a tall wooden door. On the front of it there was a carving of an eagle holding a clock in its talons. It also had a large brass doorknob. Naturally, the door was locked.

"We need Meghan," Keith said.

"Really?" Tobias said, pretending to be offended. He reached into his pocket and pulled out the homemade key he had kept beneath the loose board in his room. It no longer worked on door number seven, but this door still had one of the old locks.

He stuck the key in and it didn't turn. He pulled it out, bent the end of the key just a bit, and then stuck it back in. The lock clicked and the door was open.

"You're like a male version of Meghan," Keith whispered. "She smells better, though."

Tobias was too scared and excited to comment about that. He pushed the door and it swung open quietly. It was dark, but there were lamps in the distance lighting up small pockets of space. Tobias couldn't see everything, but he noticed dozens of beds up against the walls.

"More dorm rooms?" Keith said, sounding disappointed.

Tobias crept down the hall between the two rows of beds. Most were filled with grown bodies that were snoring. At the far end of the long room, there was an orderly with thick black hair sitting behind a desk with his head lying on his arms. He too was snoring.

"I don't like how this place feels," Keith said.

"Is there any part of Witherwood that you like the feel of?"

"That swimming pool felt okay, and I like the pudding."

"Oh, yeah, we need to talk about that."

Hanging from the end of each bed was a chart with graphs and lines on it that Tobias didn't understand. The chart closest to him had *78435 Kristin* written across the top of it.

Someone three beds down coughed and turned over. He began to moan and Tobias could see the orderly with the black hair lifting his head. Tobias and Keith dropped to the ground as the orderly stood up. Tobias scooted beneath one of the beds while Keith scooted beneath another.

The person moaning moaned louder. His raspy voice sounded old and dry.

"I'm coming!" the orderly yelled. "Hold on."

The man moaned until the orderly arrived and gave him something to drink. Tobias could only see the orderly's feet, but he could hear every word he spoke.

"Drink up. It'll help you sleep. You should be comfortable during your last days here."

After giving him a second drink, the orderly walked away.

Tobias slipped out from beneath the bed and crouched down to see where the black-haired man had gone. Thankfully he was back at his desk resting his head once more. Tobias motioned for Keith to come out. Together they moved quietly in the opposite direction, passing the door they had come through and exploring more of the third floor.

It wasn't the most surprising exploration due to the fact that there were just more beds and more people sleeping everywhere. Under the lamplight some of the sleeping people were easy to see, and all of them looked at least ninety years old.

"I had no idea this place was for old people too," Keith whispered. "I thought it was just a reform school for bad children."

"I don't get this place," Tobias said. "These people don't need education; they need funerals."

Near the northeast corner of the third floor, Tobias and Keith found what looked to be an elevator. It had a copper door and, on the wall next to it, a single button with a down arrow.

"So that's how they get these old people up here," Tobias said.

"And it's made of copper. Himzakity would like that."

"He'd be baffled by it," Tobias said. "I wonder where this elevator comes out on the first floor. It must be somewhere behind the library."

"We could press that button and find out," Keith suggested.

As tempting as it sounded, Tobias knew it was a bad idea. "They'd hear us for sure. Let's get back to the stairs and off the third floor."

"I'm all for getting out of here," Keith said. "Who knew this place could get creepier?"

The two boys walked slowly back to the stairs. Pockets of amber lamplight fought off the dark in spots, but it still wasn't easy to see everything. The floor was carpeted, and the ceiling was low with thick beams of wood crossing it every ten feet. Witherwood was a place of confusion and fright, but the third floor had a feeling all its own. It was softer, and almost homey in a weird way.

They reached the stairs and Keith pulled the door open. Tobias stepped back to make room for the opening door. As he moved, his hand knocked the end of the nearest bed. The hanging chart rattled, and Tobias grabbed it to stop it from making noise.

"Quiet," Keith mouthed.

As Tobias let go of the chart, he could just make out what was printed on top.

79235 Archie

Tobias's knees buckled and he stumbled backward.

"Shhh," Keith said, seriously this time.

Tobias reached out for the chart and looked at it closer.

79235 Archie.

Keith looked at the chart and shivered. "There are other people in the world named Archie."

"I know," Tobias replied while tiptoeing closer to the front of the bed.

"What are you doing?" Keith hissed. "We should go."

There wasn't a lamp next to the bed, but there was enough

light from a distant lamp to see what he was doing. Tobias grabbed the top of the blanket and pulled it back. Whoever was sleeping in the bed coughed slightly. Although the face was much, much older, the deep green eyes that stared at Tobias were the same—it was Archie.

I don't care who you are, you would have screamed too.

CHAPTER 14

A Piece Is Popped In

Perhaps we should take a moment to breathe. In and out. After all, we need to remember that most things pass. Bad days fade and even the most painful cuts heal. Sure, things can get heavy, but it's important to stop and realize that, in time, that clerk who was mean to you will get ill, and that crossing guard who doesn't wave at you will move away, and that flight attendant who won't give you extra peanuts—well, she's just doing what she's told—so breathe. Don't let things frighten you. It's not as if you are reading a book about two children who are trapped in a school and one of them is brainwashed and the other has just discovered that their friend has aged rapidly overnight. Oh . . . sorry, I forgot that's exactly what you are reading. Still, it wouldn't hurt to take a moment and breathe.

In and out.

Keith slapped his hand over Tobias's mouth and pulled him back through the door and onto the thin stairs. He closed the door quietly, hoping the orderly would think Tobias's scream had come from one of the old people in the beds.

Tobias was still freaking out. Keith had his hand over Tobias's mouth, but that didn't stop him from convulsing and hyperventilating.

"Did you . . . ?" Tobias tried to speak.

"I did," Keith replied. "Let's get somewhere safe."

He pushed at Tobias, moving him down the stairs. At the bottom, he yanked up the flap on the tapestry. Tobias knelt and Keith pushed him through the opening and into the hall with his foot. He then scrambled right behind. Pulling down the tapestry to hide the hole, Keith jumped up and dashed toward the library. When he got to the library door, he noticed he was alone. Tobias had not followed. Running back to the tapestry, he found Tobias sitting on the floor looking dazed.

"You're going to have to act nuts some other time." Keith grabbed the collar of Tobias's shirt and yanked him up. "We have to get out of here before someone comes."

Tobias followed this time. They entered the library, passed the boxes and counter and books, and opened the secret shelf in the back corner. Once they were in the wall, Keith slid the panel shut and they took a moment to stand in the dark and wonder about what they had seen.

"It can't be him, right?" Tobias asked.

"It seems impossible, but what I saw makes me think it was," Keith said, flipping on his flashlight.

The space behind the wall was stuffy. Tobias could feel his own hot breath as he spoke. "He was swimming just last night. He was young."

"Maybe he's just wrinkled from the water," Keith said, desperately trying to find an explanation. "You know, like how your fingers get when they've been soaking."

Tobias stared at him.

"Can you come up with a better explanation?"

"No," Tobias admitted. "Do you think all those old people are just kids who were once students here?"

"I don't know what to think. How can someone be young one day and then as old as dirt the next? I mean what's the point? Why would this be happening?"

"Okay, okay." Tobias took a deep breath. "There has to be an explanation, but I would rather figure it out or hear that explanation outside of Witherwood in the safety of a completely different place."

"Agreed. It's all about getting out," Keith said, repeating Tobias's line. "But in case you forgot, we have no way to get out."

"Fine. Tomorrow we are taking things into our own hands. If we can't get out, we'll bring the world in."

Both of them were silent.

"For the record," Keith finally said, "that was probably your best ending line yet."

They both returned to their rooms and tried with very little success to get some sleep.

CHAPTER 15

THE FOG ROLLS OUT

C harlotte was dreaming of swings and sunlight and folding paper frogs when she was awakened by the sound of crying. She opened her eyes to take in the dark. The night was in full swing with no sign of morning. The large dorm room was quiet. She rolled over on her right side to look out the windows. Most of the long purple curtains were closed, but one of the high windows was naked. Through the glass she could see nothing.

She smiled because her brain told her to.

On the lower bunk, Sue weakly cried. It was an unusual thing to hear crying in the dorms. Everyone had glazed brains, so crying was something that just didn't happen. Surprised by the sound, Charlotte rolled over and hung her head down to look at Sue.

"Are you crying?"

"I think so," Sue said.

"Are you happy?"

"I'm not sure."

Charlotte flipped around and slid off her top bunk. Sue moved her legs and Charlotte sat down.

"Ms. Ratter was just here," Sue said.

"In the middle of the night?"

"She'll be right back."

"That's nice."

"She said I'm going somewhere."

"She's really helpful," Charlotte reminded Sue.

"I know, but I don't think I want to leave. This is where I should be."

"She's not taking you from Witherwood, is she?" Charlotte asked with concern. "She wouldn't do that."

"I don't know where she's taking me. I guess that might be why I'm crying."

The sound of someone with big feet could be heard coming nearer. Ms. Ratter stopped in front of Charlotte and Sue's bunk and folded her hands in front of her.

"It's time," she announced. "Get your stuff."

"I don't have any stuff," Sue said nicely.

"Good," Ms. Ratter replied. "What is she doing on your bed?"

"Charlotte heard me crying."

"I hope they are tears of joy; you're getting a great opportunity."

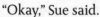

"Okay," Sue said.

"Will she be coming back?" Charlotte asked.

"You shouldn't even be awake. Get in your bed."

"Sorry." Charlotte quickly climbed to the top of the bunk and lay down.

"Good-bye, Charlotte."

"Good-bye."

Ms. Ratter put one of her cold hands on Sue's right shoulder and escorted her out of the room. Charlotte lay there with her eyes closed and her mind trying to make sense of what was happening. She folded a small piece of paper over and over in her hands. Her breathing finally began to slow, and she entered a deep sleep.

It wouldn't last long, however.

Mere minutes after she had dozed off, someone shoved her hard from the side and sent her flying from her top bunk and down onto the floor.

Charlotte saw stars and flashes of unorganized light. She wanted to scream, but the shock of what had just happened was choking her voice. Lying on the floor, she saw the shadow of someone climbing on her bed. Before she could guess who or what it might be, the shadow jumped from the bed and landed squarely on the toes of her right foot. Charlotte's body arched as she shot up. She opened her mouth to do some screaming, but a hand covered it and pulled her tightly. Charlotte struggled and thrashed, but whoever was holding her was too strong.

"Shhh," her assailant whispered. "We don't want to wake up anyone else."

Charlotte knew it wasn't her brother holding her because the hands were smaller and didn't smell bad. She also knew the voice wasn't right. But most important, Charlotte knew things. The shock and pain had been so sudden and so sharp that her brain had begun to clear quickly.

The fog was drifting.

One by one the proper memories and ideas she had once known filled up her gray matter. Charlotte stopped struggling.

"Are you okay?" the voice finally asked.

Charlotte calmly nodded her head.

The hand over her mouth dropped, and Charlotte spoke in a whisper.

"Who are you?"

"That's not important. Do you know who you are?"

"I do. I'm Charlotte Eggers, and I'm angry at you. Really angry."

"Good," Meghan said.

Charlotte was let go. She turned and sat down on the lower bed. Looking at her attacker, she spoke. "I don't understand; do I know you?"

"Now you do. I'm Meghan. I know your brother."

"Tobias," Charlotte said with relief. "Where is he?"

"He should be visiting the third floor."

"On purpose, or is he being forced to visit?"

"On purpose," Meghan answered as her long dark hair hung loosely in front of her face.

"So he's okay?"

"Let's hope so," Meghan said. "The real person you should be concerned about is Sue."

"Who?"

"The girl who was just sleeping in that bed."

Charlotte looked at the bed she was sitting on. "I don't remember any girl."

"She was just taken by Ratter."

"Who?"

Meghan rubbed her forehead and sighed. "Ms. Ratter's our headmistress. She oversees all the girls in the dorm. She's cold and calculating and evil. She's taken three girls off to another part of the school. That's why I shoved you off your bed. I told your brother I'd keep an eye on you, and if she does come for you, I want you to be clearheaded enough to know what's going on."

"Thanks," Charlotte said sincerely. She stood up and noticed Meghan was at least two inches taller than her. "So are we going after Sue?"

Meghan looked wounded. "No. We need to stay in our beds in case Ratter comes back. I have no idea where Sue was taken. And if we got caught looking for her, we'd be in more trouble than she is. So for now try to sleep. Tomorrow we'll meet up with your brother and the others."

"There's others?"

"Patrick and Keith. They're both clearheaded like us."

Charlotte climbed up on her bed and looked back down over the edge. "I know I should feel horrible about being in such an awful spot, but for some reason I feel hopeful. I just can't believe there are others like you who want out."

Meghan smiled and her eyes shone. "That's what your brother said."

"I really hope he's okay."

"Me too," Meghan replied. She then pushed her long hair back over her ears, turned around quickly, and made her way to her bed twelve bunks down.

As Charlotte lay in bed, her ears twitched. She had been under the fog of Marvin's voice ever since she was brought back just over three days ago. Now, with a clearer head, her super hearing power was coming back. She could hear the sound of singing in the next room.

Charlotte plugged her ears and tried to fall asleep.

CHAPTER 16

Plan T

T obias didn't sleep a wink. The image of an elderly Archie played over and over in his head like a horrible movie he couldn't turn off or even turn down. It seemed impossible, but he had seen it with his own eyes. Still missing all the answers, he began to mentally piece together what might be happening.

"They find kids all over the world, bring them in, muck up their brains, and treat them mean. Then they let them go for a swim. Afterward, they age quickly and then Witherwood secretly takes care of them on the third floor. Not a really smart or sensible evil plan. Oh yeah, and they feed us pudding."

Tobias tossed and turned on his cot. He stared at the wooden window and wanted to scream. Instead, he carefully wrote down all the things he had learned in the last few hours. He also began to brainstorm about a way out.

At 6:00 a.m. on the dot, Ms. Gulp unlocked door number seven and came stomping in. Tobias was lying on his cot, pretending to be dumb. It was the beginning of another day at Witherwood, but this day was going to be much different. Tobias knew that time was not on his side—new students were coming and that meant that something was going to happen to the current ones.

Luckily for all involved, Tobias had a plan.

Ms. Gulp pulled him off the cot, yelled at him until he was ready, and then escorted him to his chores.

While in the kitchen helping to make breakfast, Tobias tried his best to catch a glimpse of what Ms. Gulp did to the pudding. He felt strongly that the secret to what was happening might be made clear if he knew what the pudding possessed.

After doing the breakfast dishes, Tobias was served a large plate of scrambled eggs, cheese-covered potatoes, and a side of pudding. He knew the pudding was bad for him, but it still took every ounce of willpower he had not to eat it. He smeared his pudding around on his plate and covered it with a napkin. Then he took his own tray back to the kitchen and washed it off before anyone could discover he had skipped the most important part of his meal.

While Ms. Gulp was taking Tobias to his class, the intercom crackled to life. Following a long, painful screech, Orrin addressed the school.

"Attention, students, this announcement is to inform you that everything is fine. I repeat, all things are well in hand here. Any problem or difficulty you think you saw over the last couple of days has been taken care of. Things are in perfect harmony at Witherwood as we focus on caring and community and character. Again, everything is fine. That is all."

"That man loves to hear himself speak," Ms. Gulp said with a self-righteous sniff. "He's four scoops of full-load."

"I think he's nice," Tobias said, making sure to sound extra dumb.

"What would you know?"

Ms. Gulp dumped Tobias off at class, where he found a seat near the front and not far from Charlotte. Tobias couldn't believe how desperately he wished to be at a real school. He wanted to raise his hand and ask a few honest questions. But here at Witherwood, even pretending to ask a question would look suspicious.

"Open your books to page 269," Professor Himzakity instructed. "Now if you will look at the first paragraph. Do we have a volunteer to read?"

Everyone's hands went up.

"Excellent. How about you," he said, pointing to Charlotte.

Charlotte stood up holding her book. Slowly she read, "There are many ways for children to serve their fellow man. Some

children volunteer at hospitals. Some children help clean up parks. The most important thing for children to remember is that they should always do as they're told."

"Aren't textbooks great?" the professor said. "Thank you, Charlotte. So, class, as she read, children must do as they are told. Nobody wants to be 'that guy.'" Professor Himzakity made air quotes with his fingers. "Nobody wants to be the person who ruins the fun we all can have when we do what we're told."

For a second Tobias wished his brain was glazed only so he couldn't understand the stupid things Himzakity was saying.

At lunchtime, food was wheeled in. More sandwiches and more pudding.

Tobias sat by Keith, pretending not to know him.

"Don't eat the pudding," Tobias whispered out of the right side of his mouth.

"What?" Keith held his hand up over his mouth to hide the fact that he was talking. "The pudding's the only thing I like about this place."

"Don't eat it."

Keith started to eat his pudding as fast as he could.

"Stop," Tobias hissed.

"I'm going to pretend I didn't hear you."

Professor Himzakity was sitting across the room. He looked up and saw Keith tearing through his pudding.

"Good job, Keith!" he shouted. "Other students could learn from your example. That's the way to eat pudding."

As soon as the professor was looking the other direction, Tobias spoke again.

"Your example? You're just eating pudding."

"I can't help it. I love this stuff."

"There's something in it," Tobias said.

"Yeah there is—deliciousness."

"Don't."

"Not listening," Keith whispered.

Keith's refusing to listen was on Tobias's mind the rest of the day. He thought about it while he was helping to prepare dinner. He dwelled on it while he was doing dishes. And he dreamed about it during the few hours of sleep he got before he had to get up and make his way to the boiler room for his eleven-thirty meeting.

He retrieved his watch, a pen, and the black key from beneath the floorboard. Then he let himself out, crossed the hall, and entered the secret space through the hidden door beneath the stairs. He made one wrong turn but corrected his mistake and soon was standing behind the metal panel on the back side of the boiler room. He slid the panel down and entered the space. Patrick and Keith were already there.

One of the boilers was hissing and another popped gently.

"I'm so glad you're here," Tobias said. "This place seems far less depressing knowing there are others."

"Don't get all mushy," Keith said. "It's already warm enough in here. We don't need everyone to start blushing."

"Where's Meghan?"

"She's always fashionably late," Patrick said, followed by a sniff. "Sometimes she doesn't show at all. It's not as easy for her to slip out of her dorm as it is for us. We haven't found a hidden passage in that room yet."

The metal panel slid down and in stepped Meghan. Right behind her was Charlotte. Tobias tried hard not to squeal.

"You're here!"

"I am," Charlotte said. "And my mind's clear."

Tobias hugged his sister.

"You're okay," he said with relief. "This is amazing. I missed you, Charlotte."

"I kinda missed you too. At least the times when I had my wits about me. The other times I didn't even know who I was."

"Did Meghan punch some sense into you?"

"No, she threw me off my bed."

"I didn't enjoy it," Meghan said. "If it had been Keith, I'd have had no problem."

The five kids sat down on overturned wooden crates. They all rapidly filled one another in. Charlotte talked about Sue.

Meghan talked about Ms. Ratter. Patrick talked about the animals. Keith talked about Patrick's annoying sniffing. Meghan talked about how Keith could use some manners. Charlotte talked about how excited she was to have others to talk to. Keith went on and on about the underground pool. And Tobias talked about the pudding.

"No," Meghan whispered. "It can't be bad for you."

"Sorry, it makes me mad too," Tobias said. "But think about it. They try to get us to eat it every chance they can. There's something in it or it does something."

"I think one of us should continue to eat it," Keith suggested bravely. "Just to see what happens. Any volunteers?"

Everyone besides Tobias raised their hands.

"None of us should eat it," Tobias warned. "I know it's hard, but until we find out what's in it, we should stay away. Fake like you eat it, but don't."

"How do you know for sure it's bad?" Meghan asked.

"I don't."

"Then maybe you're wrong," Keith debated.

"He's probably not." Patrick spoke up. "I love that stuff too, but when you think about it, they're feeding us a lot of it."

Patrick stopped talking to sniff and think.

Tobias stopped thinking to talk. "Let me tell you something that might make you want to never touch that pudding again.

Keith and I made it to the third floor last night." He paused as if waiting for them to applaud. When it was clear nobody was going to, he went on. "Keith, have you told them?"

Keith shook his head. "This is the first moment I've been with Patrick when there wasn't an orderly around."

"The third floor is filled with old people," Tobias whispered above the chuffing of the boilers. "*Really* old people. There were rows of them sleeping."

"Why?" Meghan asked. "Is this like a nursing home too?"

"I don't think so," Tobias answered. "As Keith and I were leaving the third floor, I saw the name of one of the old people. Archie."

"Archie's up there?" Charlotte said, sounding hopeful.

"I think he is. And you might not believe this, but he looks like he's ninety years old."

"At least," Keith said somberly.

"That's impossible," Meghan argued. "No one can age overnight. Maybe it was his grandpa."

"It was Archie," Tobias said with certainty.

Everyone was quiet.

"I don't understand," Charlotte said. "How long was I under the influence of Marvin's voice?"

"We were brought back here four days ago," Tobias said. "So definitely not for eighty years. Here's what I think. I think they're feeding us pudding and it's somehow helping to steal our youth. I don't know how. Maybe it has something to do with the swimming pool."

"Why are they doing this?" Meghan asked.

"I'm not sure, but I think it's connected to the Gothiks. They're stores of some kind and they must be selling something there."

"What?" Charlotte questioned.

"I'm not sure."

"We've really got to get out of here," Keith said anxiously.

"Even worse," Tobias continued. "Fiddle told me that Catchers located all over the world are bringing in a bunch of new students, so Witherwood has to get rid of the current ones."

"Maybe you should have left me brainwashed," Charlotte said, half joking.

After a few moments of silence, Tobias spoke.

"I know it all seems heavy, but I have a plan."

Patrick, Keith, and Meghan seemed excited. Charlotte not so much.

"Is it like your plan when you tried to have us climb that ladder over the roof?"

"No, it's way riskier."

One of the boilers bubbled.

"Does it involve gravy, or ruining our lives?" Charlotte asked.

"It's just that your track record for plans is not that impressive. Actually, it's the opposite of impressive."

"Umpressive?" Keith asked.

Charlotte stared at Keith as he pushed his glasses up. "I don't think that's a word."

"Me neither," Keith admitted.

"Maybe we should just let Tobias tell us his plan," Meghan suggested. "I don't hear anyone else suggesting anything."

"Right," Patrick said. "Let's hear what you've got."

"I always like it when other people come up with the plan," Keith admitted. "That way, when it fails, we can blame someone besides me."

Tobias looked at Charlotte.

"Fine. You're my brother, so what choice do I have?"

"Thanks for believing in me." Tobias smiled. "All right, here's what we're going to do. We're going to start a fire."

Everyone stared blankly.

"I can hardly wait to blame you," Keith said.

"Thanks, Keith. Meghan, do you think you can get me some matches?"

Meghan nodded.

Tobias rolled up his sleeves and began talking.

CHAPTER 17

UM . . .
JUST ONE MORE QUESTION

Ralph Eggers had gotten a good night's sleep. He had also had a nutritious breakfast that consisted of some fruit and a bowl of oatmeal. He had showered, shaved, and put on a clean shirt he bought yesterday afternoon. He felt like he was getting dressed up for a job interview, or to meet someone important, when in reality he was just following up on the most interesting lead he had found yet. He was going back to Witherwood to ask a few more questions.

Finding that photo at the garage sale had been both unsettling and eerie. Ralph still had no idea what it meant, but in his heart, he felt like it had to mean something. There was always the chance that it was all a coincidence, but it seemed more fateful than that.

Ralph walked out of the YMCA where he was staying. It was a

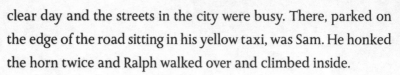
clear day and the streets in the city were busy. There, parked on the edge of the road sitting in his yellow taxi, was Sam. He honked the horn twice and Ralph walked over and climbed inside.

"Ready?"

"I am," Ralph said. "Thanks again."

"Stop thanking me," Sam insisted. "In fact, don't thank me again until we find out who you are, or I get tired of this and stop driving you around. You're not making me do anything I don't want to do."

"Well, tha— I mean, good."

Sam maneuvered the taxi through the city streets and onto the freeway and out into the lonely desert. After about thirty minutes, he took the ranch exit and continued down a smaller highway. A couple of miles later, they turned and passed the large sign on the side of the road.

Witherwood.

They could see the mesa sticking straight up in front of them as they drove closer. Near the base of the mesa, the road became steep and stitched back and forth, climbing upward. On one side of the road there was red rock, and on the other side just a drop.

"I would hate to take this road at night," Ralph said seriously, having no clue that one time he had—the time he skidded, crashed, and lost his memory. He also had no clue that if he were to climb down into the tree-covered ravine below the mesa, he would find his car, turned upside down and now covered in silt from the running river.

"This is not a good place," Sam said. "I wish that photo you found was leading us back to something more pleasant. I didn't like school growing up, and I definitely don't like this one."

The road straightened out as they reached the highest surface of the mesa. In the distance, Ralph could see the top of the iron gate. The road became level and the gate seemed to tower over the car as they pulled up.

On each side of the iron gate were thick brick pillars. The brick wall attached to the pillars ran off in both directions, looking like a slightly smaller version of the Great Wall of China. There were large weeds growing wildly at the base of the wall, and on the right pillar there was a plaque.

WITHERWOOD REFORM SCHOOL
CARING, COMMUNITY, AND CHARACTER
SINCE 1805

Hanging on the gate was a small metal sign that read:

CLOSED FOR TESTING.

"What does that mean?" Ralph said.

"I think it's pretty clear. They're closed—for testing."

Ralph got out of the car and shut the door. The wind was blowing and he could see for miles in most directions. The top of the mesa felt like a giant fingertip and he was standing on it. Sam got out of the car and stretched.

"How did we get in last time?" Ralph asked.

"The gate was open, remember? There was a truck dropping something off. We just followed them in."

Walking up to the gate, Ralph reached out and grabbed hold of two of the bars. He pulled and tugged, but the gate didn't budge.

"How do you close an entire school for testing? I mean, are the students still here? Is the faculty around? What kind of testing?"

"I do look brilliant," Sam said. "But there are some things I don't know the answer to. And those questions are some of those things."

Ralph pushed his face up to the bars. He could see the very top of the school in the distance and behind some trees.

"Someone's got to be in there. Try honking."

Sam shrugged. "Why not?"

He reached in his car window and pressed against the horn. Birds shot from the trees as the noise echoed through the air. Up on the mesa, the sound of the horn seemed lonely and forlorn. Sam honked ten more times.

As the noise drifted away, he spoke. "I really hope you're not connected to this place. It feels unnatural here."

"Honk some more," Ralph said, his face still pressed against the bars and his eyes scanning the school.

Sam blew the horn ten more times.

"Anything?" Sam asked as the sound of wind took over for the sound of the horn.

"Yes. I think someone's coming."

Sam stepped up to the bars and looked in. A person in a white lab coat was making his way down the cobblestone path toward the gate. As the person got closer, Ralph recognized Orrin from having talked to him the last time he was here. From a distance Orrin looked upset, and he was carrying something over his right shoulder.

"Hello!" Ralph called out. "It's me! I was here a few days ago."

Orrin moved closer, but he didn't look any happier.

"I know you're closed," Ralph said loudly. "Sorry, I just have a few questions."

Orrin was twenty feet away. It was clear now to see that not only was he unhappy, he was carrying some sort of antique tranquilizer gun over his shoulder.

Ralph and Sam took a couple of steps back.

Orrin walked up to the bars. "You might have noticed the sign. We're closed for testing."

"I see that," Ralph said. "But I have a couple of questions. It won't take a second."

Orrin grimaced.

"I have a first question," Sam blurted out. "What's with the gun?"

Orrin lifted the gun off his shoulder and looked at it as he held it in both hands. It was old and the stock was elaborately carved out of wood.

"It's a tranquilizer gun. We've had a little problem with mountain lions. I'm taking a great risk even being out here. But when someone leans on their horn repeatedly, I feel I have to at least investigate."

Ralph wasn't really listening. He pulled the photo from his front shirt pocket and unfolded it.

"When we were here before, you showed me two of the students you work with."

"Yes, I remember. Two of our toughest. Such a sad situation. And...?"

"And while we were in the city, I found this picture in a frame at a yard sale."

Ralph handed the picture to Orrin. Orrin looked at the picture closely and then flipped it over and read the names on the back.

"I don't think I understand what the connection is," Orrin said through the bars.

"I think they're the same kids."

Orrin studied the picture again. "I don't believe so. But if they are, that wouldn't surprise me. I think I remember hearing that they were from the city."

"I thought you said your students were brought in from all over."

"I might have, and that'd be true. But we do receive some from within the state. And I believe these two were from the city."

"I thought you said they weren't the same kids," Sam asked suspiciously.

"Well, I don't believe they are."

"Can I come in and see them again?" Ralph asked.

"I don't think so," Orrin said. "They are of no concern to you. Besides, the boy has been returned to his home."

"In the city?"

"No, his family lives elsewhere now."

"Where?" Sam challenged.

"I can't divulge that information."

"Listen," Ralph said desperately. "This is really important. I know it's not how you usually handle things, but it's all I have to go on. Do the kids have a last name?"

"I can't say."

"Please," Ralph begged.

"Fine, it's Burkenfield. But you didn't hear it from me."

"Thank you. You don't know how—" Ralph stopped talking and his eyes widened. "What was that?"

Orrin spun quickly to see what Ralph was looking at. There was nothing but the cobblestone path and trees. "What was what?"

"I think I saw something moving behind those trees," Ralph said.

Orrin pointed the tranquilizer gun in that direction.

"It must have been that mountain lion," Orrin said nervously. "I need to get inside. Good luck with your quest. I'd say I'd be happy to help you further, but there's nothing else I can offer. And I'm not particularly happy at the moment."

"Wait," Ralph insisted. "That picture might have been dropped off by a woman named Martha. Are you positive you don't have any Marthas here?"

"I'm positive of two things," Orrin said, bothered. "I'm positive that there's no one named Martha here, and I'm positive that you should leave immediately. How much help can a man give? Because I have given you more than a fair share. Now, good day!"

Orrin turned and started a weird-looking jog back to the school.

"Can you imagine him at a party?" Sam asked. "Everyone would leave."

Ralph and Sam got into the taxi and began the drive down the steep switchbacks.

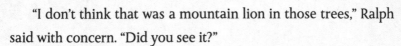

"I don't think that was a mountain lion in those trees," Ralph said with concern. "Did you see it?"

"I didn't see anything," Sam admitted. "I was too busy wishing that guy would stop talking so we could get the heck off this mesa. Did you see him? His eyes are two different colors. Something's wrong with the water here."

"I don't know about the water, but I know what a mountain lion looks like, and that didn't look anything like one. I think it had feathers."

"Listen, Lumpy. This is a dead end. It was weird finding that picture, but it was just a coincidence."

"It could be more," Ralph said. "I got a last name."

"It's probably not connected to you. I hate to say—"

Sam slammed on the car's brakes as he swerved to miss an animal darting across the road. He safely swerved back and continued driving.

"Wow. That'll make your heart race."

The two grown men took a moment to breathe.

"What'd you almost hit?"

"I'm not sure, but it wasn't a mountain lion."

"Let's get out of here."

Sam drove the taxi swiftly down the mesa and away from Witherwood.

CHAPTER 18

TASTY DETECTIVE WORK

Waiting is the worst. Waiting for a train, waiting for your break, waiting for a movie, waiting for your waiter (which is sort of ironic), waiting for the seasons to change, waiting for your life to begin, waiting for this sentence to end.

Waiting stinks.

Some people wait for the mail. Some wait for a better world. Others seem to be waiting for the world's end. We all have to wait at certain points in our life. I can't wait until that's not the case. Of course, there are always those weirdos who enjoy waiting. That man who loves long lines. That woman who hopes Christmas will never arrive. That child who would watch commercials all day while waiting for his favorite show to start. I just don't understand people sometimes.

Wait, maybe that's what makes life so interesting.

For Tobias, the worst part about Witherwood was the waiting. Now that he had a clear mind, things seemed long and tedious. And since he was monitored constantly during the day, he had to wait (there's that word) until everyone was asleep at night to ever get anything important done. So while preparing food and doing dishes, he had to grit his teeth, play dumb, and count the seconds until he would be returned to his room.

Today was particularly painful, because Tobias had a plan and he wanted to act on it. Unfortunately, his plan required him to do a few things first, and he couldn't do those things during the day while every Gulp and Himzakity was watching him like an Orrin.

Tobias went through his routine, working on breakfast, going to class, eating sandwiches at lunch, and spending the rest of the day listening to Himzakity talk about bad children becoming something good. The worst part was that there was never an opportunity to see Charlotte or his friends. So, like usual, the long day had no bright spots.

At the end of the school day, Tobias was brought back to the kitchen to help with dinner. As he worked, he struggled with playing dumb, and he also struggled with the desire to forget what he knew about the pudding and just eat it anyway.

Today the staff had been serving extra-large doses of the dessert, and Tobias had brought hundreds of cans up from the kitchen cellar. The ingredients listed on the can looked normal, but Tobias knew that Ms. Gulp always mixed something extra in.

One of the things Marvin's voice did to a person's brain was to make them lose all curiosity. So Tobias knew that the moment he began snooping around, it would look suspicious. He decided to play superdumb as he was helping the staff prepare the dinner. He brought up ten more cans of pudding and gave them to Ms. Gulp. She took the cans to a small room on the side of the kitchen. After waiting a few moments, Tobias took a deep breath and then walked directly into the small room while pretending to look for something.

Ms. Gulp spotted him immediately.

"What are you doing in here?" she barked.

"I'm fine."

"I didn't ask how you were. Now out."

"Okay." Tobias just stood there with a smile on his face, staring at Ms. Gulp.

"You've got the brain capacity of a marble."

Tobias tried to take in everything he could without moving his head or looking interested. He could see Ms. Gulp standing over a large metal bowl filled with pudding. There were empty pudding cans all over and a large black glass jar near the bowl. Tobias let his jaw go slack to look even less intelligent.

"I don't know why I bother telling you anything," Ms. Gulp said with disgust. "What's the point of talking at someone so dim? It's like talking to a Paul. Here, stir this."

Ms. Gulp handed Tobias a long wooden ladle and moved aside.

"Mix it until I tell you to stop."

Tobias started to mix. He turned his arm in a clockwise motion over and over again.

Ms. Gulp picked up the black glass jar and walked over to the wall, where she placed it in a cabinet and then locked the cabinet door. Tobias slowed his stirring as he watched her.

"Stir faster," Ms. Gulp commanded.

Tobias stirred like the wind.

"It's amazing what Marvin's voice does to you children. They should broadcast his voice over the world, get every brat to fall in line."

Tobias smiled as he stirred.

"I could say anything and you'd do it."

"Yes," Tobias said happily.

"Stick your hand in that pudding."

Tobias did exactly as she ordered. He stuck his right hand deep into the large bowl of pudding. The cold chocolate pushed up through his fingers and covered his wrist. He was confident that he was breaking some sort of health code, but as far as orders went, it could have been worse.

"Stir."

Tobias moved his hand in a clockwise circle, stirring the pudding.

The smell was fantastic!

"What a dolt," Ms. Gulp said, laughing. "A real fool. Eat a handful."

Tobias was both sad and happy about the new command. He knew there was something bad about the pudding, but he had missed the dessert. Cupping a large fistful, he brought some chocolate treat up to his face and sloppily pushed it into his mouth.

Ms. Gulp giggled.

"Take some and smear it in your hair!"

It seemed like a waste of perfectly delicious pudding. But Tobias did as he was told. He took a giant handful and plopped it on top of his head. He smeared it around, smiling.

Ms. Gulp loved it.

"What a dumb kid," she hooted. "Now hum something."

Tobias began to hum "Twinkle, Twinkle, Little Star." He had never felt more idiotic, but he knew that if he said no or stopped obeying, she might take him back to Marvin.

"Do a little dance!" Ms. Gulp clapped like she was a child who had just received the Christmas present she had always wished for. "A little dance!"

Tobias hummed and swayed. It was not his finest moment.

"Eat more pudding!"

Tobias hummed and swayed while shoving pudding into his mouth. It tasted great, but it was still an embarrassing moment.

Ms. Gulp was bent over laughing. Her red hair was spilling out of its clips and her square body was shaking like a package of fatty Jell-O. She stamped her feet in little circles and acted as if she had never in her entire life had so much fun.

Tobias was covered in pudding. The stuff in his hair was dripping down his head and back, and the pudding that had missed his mouth was covering his neck and chest. It looked like he was wearing long, dark, fancy gloves on both of his hands. He resembled a dancing pudding pop that had melted and then exploded.

Ms. Gulp was crying with laughter.

"You are so bum," she wailed incorrectly. "When the universe was passing out brains, you thought they said pasta."

It was at this moment that Orrin walked in. He took one look at Tobias and slapped his hands to his cheeks in disgust. Ms. Gulp tried unsuccessfully to stop laughing.

"What are you doing?" Orrin demanded. "He's not even supposed to be in this room."

"Don't worry about him," Ms. Gulp said, trying to catch her breath. "His brain is so gooey, he'll do whatever you say."

Tobias continued to dance and hum.

"This is highly inappropriate," Orrin pointed out.

Orrin's statement almost made Tobias laugh. Witherwood was a school that captured children, brainwashed their minds, fed them suspicious food, and aged them. And Orrin thought the pudding dance was over the line?

"Lighten up, old man," Ms. Gulp said. "This is my kitchen and he loves it. Just look at him."

Tobias continued to hum and dance.

Orrin's shoulders relaxed. "He really is under Marvin's spell, isn't he?"

"Completely. Watch this. Stick your head in that bowl."

Tobias bent over and stuck his head directly into the large bowl of pudding. It squished up around his ears and covered his eyes. He kept his head in the bowl until he was told to take it out.

"Now you tell him to do something."

"Fine," Orrin said, still acting as if the whole situation was a bit beneath him. "Recite the alphabet."

"*A, b, d, c, e, f, g, h, i, k, j, l, m, n, o, p, q, s, r, t, u, v, w, x, y, z.*"

"I should have known you'd ask him to do something boring," Ms. Gulp complained.

Orrin was offended. "Well, we shouldn't be doing this at all. Look at all the pudding you've wasted. You know how important each serving is these days. The children won't be ready for extraction unless they have the proper dose."

It was working. Tobias was covered in pudding and still quietly reciting the alphabet aloud, and Ms. Gulp and Orrin were so convinced of his brainwashing that they were talking freely in front of him.

"I put extra in the batch," Ms. Gulp said. "They are getting at least twice the amount they usually get."

"You mean extra in that pudding?" Orrin asked while pointing his bony white finger at Tobias.

"It's still good," she insisted. "What they don't know won't hurt me. Besides, there's plenty more. I know what Marvin wants, and I know we must have all students extracted before the new group arrives. I'm aware of what's on the line, Orrin."

"Good, because we will have our biggest payoff this season. The money will be phenomenal. We'll be wealthy enough to buy the very product these children are making."

"Good. I don't spend my days making meals for these ungrateful brats just to retire old and poor. I do it because I want to retire to my own private island where there are no children and nothing but servants bringing me food and drink."

"Our brand is growing," Orrin said. "There will be a well-stocked Gothik hidden in every major city soon. The rich will have access to our product like never before. Of course, that can't happen if you're smearing pudding over all our students."

Tobias was still repeating the alphabet incorrectly.

"Will you knock it off?" Ms. Gulp ordered. "See, he's as dumb as a plastic post. Now leave. I need to get dinner ready and I have a new batch of pudding to make."

Tobias stood still, hoping she would make the pudding with him in the room. He still had not seen or heard what the secret ingredient was.

"Oh," Ms. Gulp added. "Take him with you. Have one of the orderlies get him cleaned up. Then get him back. We've got children to feed."

"Come," Orrin said.

Tobias followed. He had gotten some pudding, which was bad, and some information, which was good. All in all, it was a pretty decent shift.

CHAPTER 19

FINDING FIDDLE

Tobias pushed at the bottom corner and then gently slid the metal panel down. He entered the dingy boiler room to find that he was the first to arrive. These were the most important moments of his day. Everything else felt fake and frightening, but meeting up with the others made Tobias feel like he was alive and that there was a possibility they could make it out. Plus, he would get to see Charlotte. His days had been much less comforting without her to tease him. He looked at his watch.

11:32 p.m.

Tobias tipped over a wooden crate and sat down. The boilers were humming weakly, like bulky robots that were overweight and in need of exercise.

The metal panel slid down. Tobias moved the flashlight to see Charlotte coming through. He tried hard not to look too pleased.

Meghan was directly behind her. He tried hard not to look pleased about that either.

"Are you okay?" Tobias asked his sister.

"I'm trapped in a school and having to travel through dark paths between walls just to get to a boiler room to talk to my brother. Yup, I'm doing great."

"Good," Tobias said, smiling. "For a moment I was worried."

"Patrick and Keith aren't here?" Meghan questioned needlessly. "They usually beat me."

"I can hear a lot of voices roaming the halls tonight," Charlotte said. "Maybe they're being extra careful."

"Maybe." Meghan reached in the pocket of her skirt and pulled out a pack of matches. "Here you are. Just like I promised. I found them in Ms. Ratter's break room."

Tobias took them from her. "You're good."

"When people think you're dumb, it's easy to fool them."

"Yeah," Tobias said. "I learned that today."

Tobias told Charlotte and Meghan the pudding story. He didn't leave a single thing out, and they didn't hold back a single muffled laugh.

"It worked. They just started talking as if I wasn't there."

The metal panel slid down and in crawled Keith. Directly behind him was . . . nobody.

"Where's Patrick?" Meghan asked.

"They took him," Keith said breathlessly. "Ms. Ratter came in and told him to come with her. I wanted to do something, but I knew if I said anything, it would just make things worse. She had at least three orderlies escorting him."

Charlotte knew it was a silly question, but she asked it anyway. "Where'd they take him?"

"Probably to the pool," Tobias said. "This is bad."

"It is," Keith said. "I should get back. If Ms. Ratter is coming in and out, I don't want to be missing."

"Good idea," Charlotte said sarcastically. "So then they can take you too."

"I don't know what to do," Keith admitted. "I'm not the leader; I'm the funny one."

"Really?" Charlotte asked.

"I'm funny," Keith said dejectedly. "Ask Meghan."

"Listen," Tobias said. "This just means we have to move faster, for Patrick's sake. I've got to find Fiddle. Keith, you go back. If you get taken, don't jump in the pool."

"Right," Keith said. "That actually makes sense, because I ate a snack a few minutes ago and I should wait at least half an hour to swim."

Keith looked at Charlotte and she smiled slightly.

"See?" Keith said. "Funny."

"Seems like bad timing," Charlotte commented.

Tobias ignored both of them. "Meghan, get back to your dorm, and if they notice Charlotte missing, say she went to the bathroom or just stall them until she gets back."

"Wait," Meghan protested. "Where's Charlotte going?"

"She's coming with me. Fiddle likes her, and her hearing is amazing. Besides, I need to keep an eye on my sister. If we find Fiddle, we'll figure out where to start the fire. Then tomorrow afternoon I'm going to find a way to make this happen."

"I hope it's not too late for Patrick," Keith said.

"That's not funny," Charlotte added.

"We can do this," Tobias said hopefully. "Every student here needs us to."

"You sound like a general leading his troops into battle," Meghan said, staring out from behind long strands of hair. "But we're not much of a troop. What happens if the fire gets out of hand, or nobody comes to put it out?"

"Then we'll meet here the next night and plan something else."

"You're stubborn," Meghan said.

"He really is," Charlotte agreed.

"Get ready to yell fire," Tobias instructed them. "We'll need chaos."

"I'm warming up my vocal cords as I speak." Keith looked at Charlotte again.

"Was that supposed to be funny?"

Keith pushed up his glasses. "I'm just saying, warming, fire . . . get it?"

"Maybe you're the misunderstood one of the group," Charlotte suggested.

"He's definitely that," Meghan agreed.

All four of them left the boiler room and headed off in three different directions.

Tobias and Charlotte took the passage behind the wall and exited beneath the stairs near door number seven. Unlocking the door, the two of them stepped in. Charlotte flipped on the light. There were still two rows of gray cots and the same walls and floor, and a boarded-up window that Charlotte didn't remember.

"What happened to the window?"

"We were both here. I'm pretty sure an animal broke through and we fought it off."

"Wow, we're brave."

Tobias went to the loose floorboard in the corner and pulled it up. He retrieved the map he had drawn and spread it out on one of the cots. There were still some gaps and holes in his drawing, but for the most part, he had a pretty good idea of how Witherwood was laid out.

"That's amazing," Charlotte said as she leaned over the map. "I don't remember it being so detailed."

"I've added a lot in the last four days. I don't know where Fiddle is. I know a couple of spots where he's not, but nothing for certain. He said he could hear music and it was on the first floor. So I'm ... I've got nothing else."

"Ms. Ratter plays music," Charlotte said. "Her office is in Severe Hall near the dorms, and she plays music all the time."

"There's also the singing staff members who patrol the halls," Tobias said. "He might have been talking about them."

"Right, and I heard Orrin whistle once," Charlotte joked. "Maybe that's what he meant."

Tobias smiled. "It's good to have you back. Maybe we should check out around Ms. Ratter's office first."

The Eggers children left the room, and this time they used the hallways to get around. Somewhere behind them, they could hear one of the singing voices. They hid behind a corner until the musical orderly passed. The song he sang was not uplifting.

If there's no way for you to learn,
Then tear it down and watch it burn.
If there's no way for you to see,
Count on no one, not even me.

Once the orderly and song had drifted away, Charlotte spoke. "He was singing about burning."

"Just a coincidence. Come on."

They made their way down Weary Hall and into Severe. Another singing voice could be heard in the distance.

"Nothing like weird singing orderlies roaming the halls," Charlotte whispered. "They really know how to make a creepy place creepier."

Taking a hallway behind the girls' dorms, they reached a set of stairs and hid beneath them.

"That's Ms. Ratter's office," Charlotte said, pointing to a yellow door with a poster of a cat on the front. "I think she likes kittens. A lot of the music she plays is about cats. I don't know what all these other rooms are. There's a bathroom down there and a room full of chairs over there, but I have no idea what's in the rest."

"A room full of chairs? How do you know that?"

"Meghan likes to explore. She took me there earlier today."

Tobias didn't know how to feel. He liked Meghan and he liked Charlotte, but he didn't necessarily like Meghan taking Charlotte places without him.

"Can you hear anything?" Tobias asked. "Use your ears."

Charlotte listened.

"Is it safe to do some real exploring?"

"I can hear a couple of girls snoring in the dorms. I can also hear one of the voices in the distance."

"What about Fiddle? Can you hear him doing something Fiddlish? Maybe he's clicking a pen, or playing with a Rubik's cube, or doing one of those other annoying things he does."

Charlotte took another moment to listen. "Unless he's the one flushing a toilet in the girls' bathroom, I don't hear him."

A brainwashed girl came out of the bathroom and walked like a zombie back toward the girls' dorms.

Charlotte bristled. "Is that what I look like when I'm messed up with Marvin's voice?"

"Yes."

"We've really got to get out of here."

"We've got to find Fiddle."

"Can you smell anything?"

"Yeah, when was the last time you brushed your teeth?"

"You're turning into Keith," Charlotte whispered as she punched her brother in the arm. "Let's just start checking rooms. I'm not sure what else we can do. We have no— What's that noise?"

Tobias and Charlotte pushed up against the wall behind the stairs and out of sight.

"What noise?" Tobias asked.

"It's a whirring sound."

"Marvin," Tobias said quietly.

Both Eggers children held their breath. Down the hall, the

whirring approached. From beneath the wide stairs, they could see Marvin on his electric cart. Walking next to him was Fiddle. Marvin had his thin red bag over his head to hide his face and his hat on over that. His strange bird, Capricious, was on his shoulder. Marvin's knotted hands were on the handlebar of his cart, and his squatty body looked hunched and uncomfortable. Fiddle looked like Fiddle.

"You must stay in your room," Marvin said to Fiddle, speaking from inside his bag.

"I can't always find it," Fiddle admitted.

"We will put locks on it tomorrow. That way you'll be perfectly safe. No more wandering."

"You're a really good uncle."

"I'm the best you have," Marvin reminded Fiddle. "You need to do as you are told. Recently you've become something of a problem. We are family, but even I have my limits."

"I will try to keep my brain in line."

Marvin and Fiddle passed the stairs where Tobias and Charlotte were hiding. They continued to hold their breath and Charlotte closed her eyes as if that would help her go unnoticed.

The cart slowly whirred by.

Fiddle turned his head to the side and looked directly at them. Tobias pushed back against the wall, hoping he could mesh with the building. Fiddle just smiled and kept walking.

Marvin's head was directed the other way, so he took no notice. The electric wagon stopped twenty feet down the hall in front of a skinny door with a triangle doorknob.

"Oh," Fiddle said with excitement. "There's my room. Did you—"

"No more questions," Marvin said with authority. "Now go in and stay put."

"Okay. So I shouldn't be worried about those other kids?"

"What kids?"

"That boy and girl."

"The ones you led outside to the tunnel?"

"Yes."

"Why should you be worried? There's no reason for you to spend any thought on them."

"But—"

"Go to sleep, Fiddle. It's late and I have much to do."

"Okay."

Fiddle grabbed the triangle-shaped doorknob and let himself into his room.

"Good night, everyone," Fiddle exclaimed.

Marvin shook his head as Fiddle disappeared behind the skinny door. "That child isn't right. Not right at all."

Marvin's cart carried him down the hall and into the dark.

CHAPTER 20

FINDING THE PROPER THING TO BURN

Many things can be hidden in the shadows. A deep, dark shadow has the potential to mask some fantastic things. I've lost a number of things in the shadows. My keys, my lunch, my wallet, my mind. The shadows can also provide an element of safety. If there's someone after you, you might try hiding in the shadows. If there's trouble heading your way, take to the shadows. And if you owe a strange man two gold bricks and an old badminton racket, for goodness' sake pay up. I don't think the shadows will save you.

Tobias and Charlotte crept from the shadows beneath the stairs. They walked quietly across the hall and approached Fiddle's door.

"Do we knock?" Charlotte asked.

Tobias answered by taking a hold of the triangle-shaped doorknob and turning it. With a click, the door opened, and behind the dark skinny door there was . . . not much.

The room was a large closet. A short bed was crammed against the wall, and there were lots of folded-up chairs next to a few bags of rock salt. There was also Fiddle, who was sitting on the bed pulling and twisting a large red rubber band. His smile covered the entire bottom half of his face. Tobias and Charlotte stepped in and closed the door behind them. With all three in the room, there was barely any space to move.

"Sorry we didn't knock," Charlotte said. "Are you aware this is a closet?"

"It does seem small."

"My uncle didn't see you under the stairs," Fiddle said, staring at them. "Maybe you two really are made up."

Charlotte shook her head. "We've been through this before, Fiddle."

"I know. That's why I think you're not just a thought. Most of the voices in my head only show up once."

Charlotte sat down on the bags of rock salt.

"You came to see me yesterday," Tobias reminded him, trying to find a place to sit.

"I remember that."

"I like your new room," Charlotte said in a kind way. "It's cozy."

"You seem more positive than before," Fiddle said to her. "That's nice. I think this room is a punishment. Plus, I don't like Ms. Ratter. Ms. Gulp was much nicer."

"What?" Tobias and Charlotte said together.

"Yeah, she left me alone and she didn't play music all the time. Ms. Ratter calls me stupid."

"You're not," Charlotte said.

"Much kinder than before," Fiddle said, grinning. "I'm really glad to see you two together. Otherwise, it doesn't look right."

"Listen, Fiddle," Tobias said. "We would love to just hang out in this closet talking, but we think bad things are happening. And we need your help."

"Last time I helped you, they moved me from my room."

"This time we want to help the whole school," Tobias told him.

"They might send me to a really crummy spot for that. What's smaller than a closet?"

"A cabinet," Charlotte said, as if they were playing a guessing game.

"They won't send you to a cabinet," Tobias promised. "We just need to ask you a question."

Fiddle fiddled with the rubber band. He lost his hold and it hit Tobias on the cheek.

"Ouch," Tobias said, rubbing his face.

"Sorry." Fiddle bent over to get the rubber band and knocked his head against Charlotte's knee.

"You need a bigger room," Charlotte said.

"You need to answer a question," Tobias pleaded.

"Okay, but only because I believe you two are good and sometimes I think my uncle isn't."

Tobias got right to it. "You said there's a spot here that would burn for days because of what's in it."

"I did?"

Charlotte rubbed her forehead. "I forgot how hard it is to get information from you."

"If you're looking for someplace that will burn for a long time, you need the barn behind the school. That's where they keep the wood and gas for some of the cars and equipment. I used to be able to go there when I was a little kid and watch the workers stack wood and use the machines. The staff used to tell me to be careful, because if the wood caught on fire, the shed would burn for days. They call it the bonfire barn. It's been a long time since I've been there."

"Do you think they use it for storage any longer?" Tobias asked.

"That's a weird question. Don't you remember we passed it on our way to the tunnel last time? It's by that old outhouse."

"I think I remember. It's far enough away from the back of the school that if it caught on fire it wouldn't get Witherwood? I don't want any of the students getting hurt."

"I think so. It's in that clearing by itself, near the outhouse."

"Perfect," Tobias said in a hushed voice. "Nobody's out there, and it would burn like a giant bonfire. Someone would have to notice it from far away. We just need a few firefighters to come up here from the real world. Once they see what's happening, we'll all be saved."

"What if the firefighters are on Marvin's side?" Charlotte asked. "That horrible sheriff is."

"We can only hope that the fire is so noticeable that at least one honest person investigates."

"Sounds like a really exciting plan," Fiddle said. "How are you going to get to the barn?"

"I'm going out a window," Tobias said. "The first-floor windows might be barred, but I know the third-floor windows aren't."

"Fun," Fiddle said. "I'm still not coming with you."

"We wouldn't ask you to."

"Well, now I kind of want to."

"Listen, all you have to do is promise not to tell a single soul that you saw us. If someone asks, you don't say a thing. Talk about trees or something. Also, tomorrow when people start yelling *fire*, run someplace safe."

"I can do that."

"Thanks, Fiddle," Charlotte said.

"Can I tell you something?" Fiddle asked, looking around to see if they were alone.

"Sure."

"I lied about my uncle. I don't wonder if he's not nice, I know he isn't."

"We know too," Tobias said.

"He's taking kids to the pool."

Tobias and Charlotte both held their breath, not wanting to startle Fiddle into losing his train of thought.

"So what happens in the pool?" Tobias asked casually.

"I'm not sure, but I'm sure it's not good. It has something to do with the mesa. There's something in the water."

"See?" Tobias said. "We have to do this."

"I won't say a word," Fiddle promised. "Unless I forget I told you I wouldn't."

"Please don't," Tobias said. "This is for every student here. It might be our one shot."

"Good luck."

"Thanks, Fiddle," Charlotte said again.

"You two are probably the nicest people I've met."

"If this works, maybe you'll get a chance to meet nicer ones."

Fiddle stopped scratching himself. "What I really want is to try skiing."

"Really?" Charlotte said.

"I think so. I mean, I don't really know what it is, I just like the word. Skiing."

Tobias and Charlotte left Fiddle in his closet alone with his thoughts. Closing the door, they slunk to the shadows beneath the wide stairs.

"I guess I'll go back to my bed," Charlotte said.

"And I get to go to my beautiful room with the lovely view of wood."

"You know this is a really crazy idea you came up with. A dangerous, crazy idea."

"I know," Tobias admitted. "But I can't think of anything else to try. Besides, crazy ideas are sort of my specialty."

"It was your crazy idea to put tadpoles in gravy that got us stuck here."

"Let's just hope *this* crazy idea gets us out."

The Eggers children split up and went their separate ways, knowing full well that tomorrow would be one frightening, dangerous, and exciting day.

CHAPTER 21

TREMORS

T he morning was bright and beautiful. The sun rose up and lit the mesa like a candle. A soft warm wind drifted in from the north along with the smell of honeysuckle and pine. Birds sang in the cedar trees and cottonwoods while their needles and leaves shimmered and danced.

Of course, Tobias couldn't see any of that due to his window being boarded up.

Ms. Gulp fetched him at 6:00 a.m. as usual. Tobias showered as usual. He brushed his teeth as usual and followed Ms. Gulp down the hall to the kitchen as usual. It was in the hallway where things began to get unusual. The school began to tremble. Pictures on the walls shook and the floor wobbled.

Ms. Gulp turned and looked at Tobias as if he were responsible for what was happening.

"It's not me!"

Looking at the shaking walls, she yelled, "Quake!"

Ms. Gulp pushed Tobias aside as she ran to take shelter under one of the door frames. Tobias did the same as the ground and hallway swayed and groaned. In the distance, he could hear others screaming and yelling. The lights flashed off and then on and then off. Although it felt much longer, the shaking was over in a few moments and everything settled as if it had never been twitching in the first place.

The lights flashed back on.

Dust from the walls and ceiling floated in the air. Tobias looked to the left and saw Ms. Gulp cowering beneath a door frame on her knees with her arms over her head. She looked like a fat crumpled box. Tobias was going to say something smart, but he remembered that he was still supposed to be dumb.

Ms. Gulp stood. She dusted off her big bosom and stomach and smoothed back her hair, acting as if she had not been the least bit frightened.

"Now," she said with a dry sniff. "Let's hope there's no significant damage to the school."

Tobias felt differently. He hoped all the walls had crumbled and that students were currently running out of the school and down the mesa. But when they reached the kitchen, he could see quite clearly that things were still a lot like they always had been.

Sure, a number of pans and jars had been shaken off tables, but the walls were still standing.

"Start cleaning things up this instant."

Tobias began to pick up pans and sweep up spills. Ms. Gulp ran around like a chicken that had been swallowed by a pig that had been swallowed by a bull. She was talking to orderlies and bossing people around with more intensity than usual. Tobias decided to use the distraction to his advantage. He cleaned up a jar of flour that had burst and then picked up all the fruit that had rolled out of their baskets and bins. He pretended to clean his way right into the small room where Ms. Gulp usually worked on the pudding. Like the others, the room was messy. There were cans on the floor and at least three spills that needed cleaning up. Tobias carefully scooted past the spills, making his way closer to the cabinet where the secret ingredient was stored. He kept his eyes and ears wide-open, listening for Ms. Gulp and pretending to clean.

There was no doubt about what Tobias was going to do later today. He was committed to starting the fire that would hopefully bring in outsiders to rescue them. But Tobias knew it might be helpful to their cause if he also had a sample of what Ms. Gulp was sticking in their pudding.

He stepped closer to the cabinet.

He could hear Ms. Gulp in the kitchen yelling at an orderly to get the stove working. A small bead of sweat rolled down the tip of Tobias's nose. The sweat surprised him. He knew he was nervous, but not that nervous.

Tobias reached the cabinet and pretended to wipe and clean right beneath it. The cabinet was locked, but it was an old cabinet with a weak lock. Tobias grabbed a potato peeler off the counter and checked to see if the coast was clear.

Nobody was coming.

Quickly, he jammed the peeler into the crack of the cabinet door near the handle and pulled it to the side. The clasp snapped and the door of the cabinet swung open. Tobias looked back.

He was still alone.

He turned, and there, sitting inside the cabinet, was a large dark container. Without wasting a second, he reached out, popped off the top, and thrust his hand inside. He grabbed a handful of whatever it was and pulled it out. He shoved the stuff into one of his front pockets as he put the lid of the jar back on with his other hand. Using his elbow, he hit the cabinet door and slammed it shut just as Ms. Gulp herself came walking into the room.

Tobias scrubbed the counter, trying to look as innocent as he could.

"What are you doing? Nobody told you to clean this room."

Tobias tried to look surprised.

"Get out of here. What is it with you? You want to leave covered in pudding again?"

"Okay," Tobias said dumbly, trying to get by her.

"Wait." Ms. Gulp stepped up to him slowly. She eyed him with her hard eyes and then scrunched her tiny mouth. "What's that on your face?"

Tobias just stood there, afraid to do anything. She smelled like glue and cough medicine.

"Are you sweating?" she asked.

Tobias smiled, knowing he looked guilty of something.

"Good," she said. "It's about time you worked hard enough to sweat. Now, go see where you can help in the kitchen. Go!"

"Okay," Tobias said again, trying to sound casual but knowing he had been seconds away from pooping his pants.

There were plenty of things for Tobias to clean up in the kitchen. In fact, there was plenty for all the students to clean up in the school. The quake had knocked countless things off tables and walls. Some kids had gotten scraped up, and a pipe had burst in Severe Hall, making it necessary to hold class in Never Hall. Orrin made three announcements over the speakers, always promising that everything was fine. And talking as if an earthquake had somehow made things better.

Tobias was okay with all the confusion. The mesa-quake was a scary distraction. The more disruptive things were to the routine, the less likely he was to be noticed or missed.

In class, Professor Himzakity was completely uneasy. He kept going over the same bits of their lesson. And at lunch, he accidentally hit his head on a desk while bending over to pick up his pencil.

"This is not my day."

Tobias smiled, knowing it was about to get worse.

The orderlies wheeled in the lunch carts, each one filled with food and drink and pudding. The two orderlies pushing the carts seemed more bothered than usual. Tobias looked out the corner of his left eye and saw Charlotte sitting four desks down. He nodded ever so slightly and she stood up.

It was time.

After Charlotte stood, Keith got up from his seat on the opposite side of the room. Charlotte walked down the row of desks toward the aisle where the carts were. Keith began walking straight down the aisle directly toward the food. When Charlotte reached the aisle, she dropped her pencil as planned. As she bent down to pick it up, Keith ran right into her. He stumbled over her and slammed hard into one of the lunch carts. The cart tipped over, crashing into the other and sending food flying everywhere. Professor Himzakity was hit in the face by a couple of sandwiches as pudding splattered against the floor and walls. Some of the students moved to pick up food or to get out of the way.

"What's happened?!" Himzakity hollered.

Meghan pointed toward Keith as he lay in the aisle next to the tipped-over cart. "He tripped."

"Clean it up!" the professor ordered. "Get some paper towels!"

Everyone began to scurry around picking things up. Some students ran to the bathroom in the hall to get paper towels. Tobias ran toward the bathroom as well, but instead of stopping, he kept running. He slipped behind a stone pillar and made sure no one had seen him. He then carefully traveled through Never Hall without being spotted.

At the corner where Weary and Never Hall met, Tobias hid behind a metal statue of two men—one man was labeled Hyrum Withers; the other had a plaque on it too, but the name was crossed out. Tobias remained hidden as four orderlies walked past going to different parts of the school. Once the coast was clear, he continued to creep.

Before he got to the cafeteria, he crouched down behind a large trash can. He knew getting past the lunchroom would be the hardest part. Once he had made it through, he could take the hallway to where the locker was that led to the library.

The cafeteria was empty.

There was no one at the long tables that Tobias himself had wiped off only hours earlier. The metal freezers at the end of the room buzzed calmly as light from the stained glass window colored the room in blues and greens and reds. Ms. Gulp and her staff were in the kitchen prepping food for dinner, but there was always the chance one of them would step out and spot Tobias walking through.

He got on all fours and scurried across the hall and behind one of the rows of tables. He crawled slowly, keeping low to the ground and remaining partially hidden by the table benches. Halfway across the cafeteria, he heard the kitchen doors swing open and someone come out. Tobias slipped farther under the bench and held his breath.

Through the legs of the table, he could see that it was Ms. Gulp. She was holding a plate of food and standing next to a woman orderly who had short hair and thin shoulders.

"This is a day to forget," Ms. Gulp complained. "This mesa makes me uneasy. Someday, the whole thing might just tip over and kill us all. Like lambs before their fathers."

"Don't say that," the thin-shouldered woman said.

"I'll say what I want," Ms. Gulp insisted. "Now you go meet Orrin in the front office and give him that list. Deliveries are coming tomorrow, and he needs to know who to let in."

The woman walked off with quick, purposeful steps. Ms. Gulp just stood there until she was gone.

"Sometimes I don't know who's more pigheaded. The children or the staff around here. Telling me what to say. That woman could use an attitude adjustment."

Tobias willed Ms. Gulp to go back into the kitchen, but he

lacked any sort of mind control. Ms. Gulp walked closer and sat down on the bench almost directly across from where Tobias was hiding. He could see the side of her brown skirt and her fat knees that looked like unbaked cinnamon rolls. She slammed her plate down on the table above Tobias and began to eat. It sounded like someone had turned on a radio and tuned it to a station that played only uncomfortable noises.

Namnamnamanammam!

Specks of food and liquid were raining down. Tobias got gravy on his elbow, which stuck out from under the bench. Ms. Gulp stopped eating to belch.

BURRRRRRRUUUUUUUP!

Her doughy knees shook as she expelled air. The noise echoed off the high ceiling of the cathedral-like cafeteria. The puffy blue animal on the stained glass window looked embarrassed to be witnessing such a thing. Ms. Gulp shifted her weight on the bench and something worse than a burp happened. Tobias would have given almost anything to plug his nose. The smell was unbearable, but he was too close to her to make any movement. His nostrils burned and he felt light-headed and sick. His throat tried to dry heave, but he bit his tongue and fought to keep it together.

Ms. Gulp continued to eat. After she was done, Tobias could hear her passionately licking her plate. She then burped again, got up, and returned to the kitchen.

Tobias didn't waste a moment. He scurried beneath the bench and across the floor as fast as he could. He wasn't as worried about getting caught as he was about getting stuck under a bench and having to watch and smell Ms. Gulp eat her second lunch.

At the end of the table, he bolted across the rest of the room and farther into Weary Hall. The dark lighting and plush carpet were a welcome sight. Keeping to the right, he maneuvered down the hall, passing door number seven and finally reaching the locker he was looking for. He popped it open and climbed inside. With a quick snap, he closed the door and exhaled.

"This better work," he said to himself. "Nobody should ever have to watch Ms. Gulp eat."

It was dark in the locker. It was also the first private moment Tobias had had since breakfast. He reached in his front right pocket and pulled out some of the stuff he had taken from the glass jar in the pudding room. He couldn't see it very well, but it was cold and grainy. It felt almost wet and smelled dirty and sour. Tobias was tempted to taste it, but his better judgment kicked in and he decided not to. He put the stuff back into his pocket and began to work his way through the dark hidden passage.

He had a fire to light.

CHAPTER 22

SOMETHING IN THE TREES

Tobias knew the passage he was moving through well. He had traveled it a few times, and even though there were some twists and turns, it was pretty much a direct route to the library.

When he reached the end of the passageway, he carefully slid the back of the bookshelf over. There was no noise or movement, so he crawled out.

It was odd to see the library in the daytime. The windows looked massive, and long arms of sunlight reached in as if they were trying to fish out handfuls of books. Tobias had done almost all his exploring and mapping in the dead of night, so to see things clearly was weird. It was also weird that it was the middle of the day and he was in the middle of a library, and nobody was there. The lights weren't even on.

It seemed sort of sad.

Tobias walked through the library and unlocked the front door. He pulled it open just enough to peek out. The halls were lit but no one was around. He slipped out the doors and down the hall to the tall tapestry with the goat stitched on it. Grabbing the bottom of the material, he pulled it up as quickly as he could. When the opening was big enough, he got on his belly and wiggled behind the material. He pulled it shut and took a moment to slow his heart rate while sitting on the narrow stairs.

"You can do this," he encouraged himself. "You don't want to be stuck here forever. And you definitely don't want to be extracted, whatever that means."

Tobias turned and climbed the stairs. At the top, the door was closed but unlocked. He twisted the knob and pushed the door out. The third-story halls were almost as dark as before. All the thick curtains were closed and the only light came from the low-glowing lamps. Down the hall, Tobias could see that the orderlies' station was vacant.

He stepped cautiously onto the third floor and his eyes went directly toward Archie's bed. Someone was still there and was snoring softly. Tobias reached for the chart hooked on the end of the bed.

79235 Archie.

Tobias knew he shouldn't, but he wanted a better look. He

stepped up to the head of the bed and bent down. The man lying there had a bald wrinkled head and twisted old ears. He looked like Archie dressed up as an elderly person. His nostrils were bigger and his cheeks fluttered as he snored.

"Archie," Tobias whispered.

The old man's eyes opened so quickly it caught Tobias by surprise. Archie just stared.

"Is it you?" Tobias asked.

Archie's eyes widened and his nostrils flared slightly.

"What happened to you?"

The old man's breathing weakened.

"Don't worry. I'll get you out of here," Tobias insisted. "I promise."

The corners of Archie's mouth flickered. "Sandwich."

"Yes, I'll bring you a sandwich."

Archie smiled. He then closed his eyes and rejoined the sleep he had previously been taking. Tobias stood up and moved from around the bed to the closest window.

He slipped behind the curtains.

In back of the curtains, he could see out into the bright sky. There were no bars on the third-story windows, and the view of the mesa was one Tobias had never witnessed before. The trees were green and the sky around the mesa stretched on for what looked like forever. He could see part of the thick brick wall that encircled the school and a small cobblestone path that ran through the vegetation below. Quietly moving his right hand, he reached for the window latch and was happy to discover there was no clasp keeping it locked. He pressed on the handle and the window slid open with ease.

A warm breeze drifted in.

As he looked down, it occurred to Tobias that he might have been talking too big when he told Charlotte he'd have no problem climbing down. Charlotte was the athletic one, and even she would have had some trouble. Tobias leaned his head out the window. He could see the bars a couple of feet down on the front of the second-story windows.

"That should make it easier," he whispered to himself.

Tobias slid the window all the way open and put one leg out. He shifted and turned, bringing his second leg out as well. His toes tried to find a tochold on the brick wall as he carefully lowered himself down. Resting on his arms, he closed the window behind him as best as he could to cover his tracks.

Tobias's arms began to burn as he straightened them out to get lower. Clinging to the bottom of the third-story window, he looked down to find that his feet were still a few inches away from the security bars on the second-story window.

His fingers and arms were on fire.

Knowing there was no way he could pull himself back up, Tobias bravely let go.

He dropped a few inches before his feet landed on the top bar of the second-story window. Tobias hugged the side of the school as if it were the mother he had lost.

Pressing his body against the building, he lowered his left foot and set it on the next bar down. Repeating the process with his right foot allowed him to get low enough to lean to his right and grab ahold of the bars with his hand. From there it was like climbing down a ladder. Fortunately, the second-story window had its curtains closed as well. If anyone had been inside and looking out, Tobias would have been spotted for sure.

Tobias hung from the bottom bar on the second window and then transferred down to the set of bars on the ground-floor windows. It was these windows Tobias was most worried about. A lot of stuff happened on the first floor of Witherwood. He knew there was a high possibility that there would be someone looking out.

He got lucky; there wasn't.

Tobias looked into the window and saw an empty room. Halfway down the first-floor window bars, he let go and jumped to the ground.

"So far, so good."

Tobias dashed into the trees. He knew that Orrin had been going on and on about how all the animals were taken care of, but he also knew that Orrin was a liar. It was true that Protectors normally didn't come out in the daylight. Still, in order for him to have the courage to move, Tobias told himself over and over . . .

"No Protectors will be out. No Protectors will be out."

He ran as fast as he could through the trees and toward the back of the school. Passing the corner, he began to move diagonally in the direction of the bonfire barn.

Tobias spotted the roof of the barn. Unfortunately, that wasn't all he could see. Darting through the trees, he saw the shadow of something unusual. His first impulse was to scream. His second impulse was to run faster.

The shadow kept up.

Tobias's legs hurt, his arms ached, and his lungs felt like two cans of gasoline that had already been lit. But, like climbing down from the windows, he couldn't stop. He had to keep going.

There was now a shadow to his right as well.

Tobias wanted one of the shadows to be Lars, but both of them were far too big to fit the small creature he and Charlotte had once befriended.

The foliage thinned and the trees opened up. Tobias saw the barn clearly. He recognized it now as one of the buildings they had passed on the night they had made their escape. It looked like an old-fashioned barn that someone might sing a children's song about. The only difference was that it was weathered and in need of a coat of red paint. It had a green roof that was collapsing in the back, and the sides were made up of thin warped boards.

Turning his head to the right, Tobias tried to get a look at what he was running with. There was nothing to the right of him. Looking left, he was equally surprised to find himself alone—surprised and relieved.

Tobias reached the barn and started to run around the back of it, looking for an entrance. He skidded to a quick stop.

Two orderlies were standing near a small tractor next to the barn. A skinny, hairy-faced one was using a wrench and working on the engine of the tractor while the skinny, pocked-faced one was standing there watching. Tobias stayed behind the corner and pushed his back up against the side of the barn. He peeked his right eye around.

The two orderlies were talking.

"I've worked here for five years and I'm still not sure about everything that happens," the pocked-faced one said.

The hairy-faced one had a response. "What's to know? They reform these kids and all we have to worry about is keeping our mouths shut."

"Right," Mr. Pocked-face said sarcastically. "That doesn't

explain the Protectors. What are those animals, and why do they want to protect this place? And what about Mr. Bag Face? He..."

The hairy one stood up quickly, holding his wrench like a weapon and shaking it at the other one. "Watch what you say. We all signed agreements when we started here. No discussion about anything that happens. In return we're all going to be very rich. I'm not losing out on a job because you can't keep your mouth shut. Where were you before you worked here?"

"I was in prison," Pock said defensively. "When I got out, I saw an ad in the paper."

"We all did," Hairy said. "Nobody without a colorful past would apply to the ad we did. We are the fortunate. We have jobs."

Tobias listened carefully. He had wondered where the orderlies came from. They were all rough-looking and rarely spoke. It was the people like Ms. Gulp and Orrin who did all the commanding and yelling.

As interesting as the conversation he was eavesdropping on was, Tobias needed to get into the barn before someone noticed he was missing.

Looking inside the barn, Tobias could see another tractor and some plastic barrels. He could also see piles of wood. He was tempted to just light a match where he was and start the barn burning from the outside, but he knew it probably wouldn't catch. Plus, there was no way he was about to start a fire until he knew for sure nobody was inside.

"This tractor's not going to run anytime soon," the hairy one said. "We should report to the office and let them know we need parts."

"Fine by me," Pock said.

Heading toward Witherwood, the two orderlies approached the corner where Tobias was hiding. Tobias pressed himself up against the wall and closed his eyes. They walked right past him without noticing. He opened his eyes and watched them disappear into the trees.

Quietly, he moved around the corner of the barn and toward the open door near the tractor. Tobias looked inside and couldn't see anyone. Moving in, he passed the second tractor and a work-bench that was covered with rusty tools and dirty rags.

Tobias looked up. Something didn't smell right.

Above him was a loft littered with stringy hay and filled with old furniture and pieces of farm equipment. The entire back wall of the shed was stacked, floor to ceiling, with logs that were dusted in spiderwebs and dirt. There were metal cans with the words PETROL and GASOLINE written on them in black marker near a wooden ladder that led to the loft. Next to the ladder there was a pair of eyes staring directly at him.

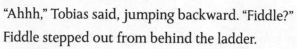

"Ahhh," Tobias said, jumping backward. "Fiddle?"

Fiddle stepped out from behind the ladder.

"I knew you'd come here. That's pretty smart of me, isn't it?"

Tobias was too busy recovering from the surprise to answer.

"I've been waiting."

"I should have recognized that smell," Tobias finally said.

"I've found that when people ask about specific things, they usually have a reason." Fiddle smiled wide. "So what are you going to do to this barn?"

"Listen, Fiddle, we have to put a stop to this school. I'm just going to send a little smoke signal so someone can come and help us."

"A little signal?" he asked, scratching at his eyebrows with the tips of his fingers.

"Yeah, you probably should leave."

"No, thank you," Fiddle said politely. "Everyone always wants me to leave. I wonder why. I don't really take up much space, and I hardly stop anyone from doing what they are doing. I usually just like being near something that's going on. It gets so . . . so . . . boring having to always stay put in my room. I'm not sure exactly how old I am, but I know I've spent too much time doing nothing. So, what I'm trying to say is that I would like to help do something."

"I'm going to light this whole barn on fire," Tobias blurted out. "It's our only chance."

"Good," Fiddle said calmly. "I wanna help."

"Last time you helped, you got in trouble, and you were moved to a closet."

"Sometimes boredom is worse than punishment."

"That's a menacing motto."

"I don't really know what a motto is," Fiddle admitted. "Is it one of those tiny fish?"

"No, and it's not important. Are you ready?"

"Ever since I was a little child and they told me that this place was filled with things that could easily catch fire, I think I've wondered what it would look like if it did. I think I'm ready to see this barn finally live up to its name."

Fiddle scratched at his eyebrows again while Tobias crumpled up a piece of the old newspaper and set it on the ground near the gas cans.

It's important to remember a few things here. Tobias wasn't bored. He wasn't doing what he was doing because he was the clever mischievous child he used to be. Nope, Tobias was doing what he was doing because a wrong needed to be righted. This was about more than just Tobias and Charlotte being cruelly dropped off by their dad in a terrible place: This was about saving the hopes and lives of every current and future student who might be unlucky enough to call Witherwood Reform School home.

Lighting a fire is a frightening thing, but sometimes it takes great effort to make changes.

Tobias nervously took out the matches Meghan had given him. He struck a match and a flame was born.

CHAPTER 23

BURN, BABY, BURN

You should never play with fire. Of course, why would you? It makes a lousy toy and your hands and eyebrows will never forgive you. Fire is an important element, but a dangerous plaything. Fire might be beautiful when you are cold and sitting around a campfire roasting marsh-mallows. But it is a problem, a plight, and a fear when you are facing it in a dangerous situation. It destroys things, consumes stuff, and will lick just about anything in its way. You would be wise to respect fire.

Please, don't fry this at home.

Tobias lifted the burning match and stared at the flame.

"I hope this works."

"What works?" Fiddle asked.

"The fire, remember? As soon as I light this paper, run for the trees."

Tobias lowered the match to the paper just as a large dark shadow blew through the open door and knocked into him from behind. Tobias fell to the ground, his body smothering the match he was holding. Before he could roll over to see what had hit him, he was grabbed by the ankles and pulled toward the door. Kicking and screaming, he saw that the assailant wasn't a person—it was an animal. It had him by the ankles with its leathery beak and was dragging him out of the barn. Fiddle just stood there scratching his wrist and watching as if it was all entertainment.

"Fiddle, help!"

"Right," he said. "I should help."

"Now!"

Fiddle glanced around. He looked more like he was playing a game of I Spy than trying to rescue someone.

"Oh!" he exclaimed. "A shovel."

Fiddle jogged to the shovel as Tobias clawed at the dirt to prevent himself from being pulled out of the barn.

Grabbing the shovel, Fiddle spun around and, with one solid clank, smacked the animal in the head. The creature screamed and rolled onto the ground with a thud. Tobias scrambled away from it and back onto his own two feet. His pants were torn where the thing had been biting down, but there was no sign of blood. He looked at Fiddle.

"This is a really nice shovel," Fiddle said, staring at the tool. "Usually shovels are old and dirty, but this one doesn't look like it's been used."

Tobias huffed and puffed. "That's great. Thanks."

"I told you I like to help."

"Do you think it's dead?" Tobias questioned as he moved a few inches closer to the creature. "I've never seen anything quite like it."

"It's definitely a Protector. They guard Witherwood."

"What is it, though? It's got a beak and talons and a wolf's body with a turtle shell."

"My uncle says they're bits of many things. But most of all they are failed experiments."

"This place should not be experimenting with anything but shutting down."

"The Protectors aren't really supposed to come out in the daytime. I heard that rat lady with the tight hair say that the shaky ground is making them act differently. They have a strong connection with the mesa. I think they are guarding something. Don't ask me what."

"Do you know what?" Tobias asked.

"What?"

"No, do you know what they're guarding?"

"Nope."

"You're always really clear about what you're saying," Tobias said sarcastically.

"Thanks."

Tobias looked down at the Protector. "So, what should we do with it?"

The animal was breathing, but it showed no other sign of life.

"I'll drag it out to the trees," Fiddle said. "You light things up."

"What if it wakes up, or what if there are others?"

"They won't harm me."

"Why not?"

"Something about my blood," Fiddle answered. "My uncle Marvin always says our blood keeps them away."

Fiddle began to drag the animal from the barn and toward the trees.

"You better run fast, Tobias. If the other Protectors see you burning parts of the school, they might not be happy."

Tobias struck another match and lit the crumpled piece of newspaper. He dropped it near the gas cans and the pile of old rags. Almost instantly, the flames began to lick and chew the dirty rags. Tobias spun around and dashed out the door. He saw Fiddle at the tree line, dragging the beast behind him.

Tobias picked up his pace and in seconds he was helping

Fiddle pull the creature into the trees and out of the open. They both knelt down and looked out toward the bonfire barn.

Nothing was happening.

"Maybe you lit it wrong," Fiddle suggested.

"I know how to light paper. I saw it catch on the rags right next to the gas cans."

"Sometimes my eyes play tricks on me," Fiddle said.

"My eyes weren't playing any tricks. I saw it burning."

"I once saw a small girl hovering in my room picking pens from my drawer."

"That was Charlotte. I was there."

"Oh, I thought she looked familiar."

"Do you see any smoke?" Tobias asked, ignoring Fiddle's drifting mind. "Because I can smell fire."

"I don't see any smoke, but I obviously can't trust my eyes. I'm going to have to—"

A small explosion rocked the air, followed by another bigger one. Tobias watched as smoke raced out of the barn door like long puffy ghosts.

"I think—"

Another explosion tore through the air, interrupting Tobias. He plugged his ears as flames shot out of the barn door and climbed the walls.

"I think you lit it right," Fiddle observed. "Sorry I doubted you."

Another explosion and now the flames were reaching the top of the barn. They heard an alarm coming from Witherwood.

"Someone's noticed," Tobias said.

"Now what do we do?" Fiddle said with excitement.

"I haven't thought that far ahead. We need to get back inside without anyone seeing us."

"I know a good way."

"Really?" Tobias questioned.

"Let's leave this Protector here, though."

"Why would we bring it?"

"Good point."

Tobias took a last look at the bonfire barn. It was truly living up to its name. Fire was consuming it like a great beast swallowing a fat piece of meat. Black smoke rose up into the air. It was a magnificent smoke signal.

"Let's hope someone sees this."

"Sees what?"

"Just get us inside," Tobias said.

Fiddle led the way.

CHAPTER 24

YELLING FOR YOUR LIFE

Charlotte was doing her best to not appear nervous. The distraction she had caused with Keith had worked perfectly. After everything was picked up and put back in its place, nobody seemed to notice that Tobias was missing. Professor Himzakity went on and on about nothing while Charlotte anxiously sat in her chair hoping that Tobias would be successful and that the plan would work. Fire was a dangerous thing, and there was a massive possibility of something going horribly wrong.

"Who knows why children are paid less than adults?" the professor asked.

Everyone raised their hands.

"Wendy," he said, picking a skinny, short girl in the back corner of the room.

"Because we're lucky to get paid at all."

"Exactly."

The suspense was almost more than Charlotte could bear. She looked over at Meghan, who was holding her knees in place to stop her legs from shaking. Keith wasn't much better. He had sweat on the side of his face and his hands were twitching.

Just as Charlotte was beginning to think that Tobias had failed, a loud alarm began to screech and wail. Everyone glanced around in confusion.

"Stay calm," Professor Himzakity said nervously. "There's nothing to worry about."

Orderlies began running past the windows toward the rear of Witherwood.

The alarm continued to whine.

Most of the students plugged their ears and began to fidget at their desks.

Professor Himzakity held up his hands, showing the class his palms. "Please, there's nothing to worry about. Nothing at all!"

Orrin's voice came on over the loudspeaker: "All students to their dorms immediately! All students to their dorms immediately."

Every eye in the classroom looked at Professor Himzakity.

"To your dorms!" he ordered.

Charlotte's hands were shaking. She could barely stand up without falling over, and her neck was turning red from her collarbone up to her chin.

"To your dorms," the professor barked. "No dawdling!"

The students pushed out the classroom door into the hall, where other classrooms were emptying their students into the ocean of kids. Everyone's brains were glossy, but they seemed to understand fear and confusion. Somewhere someone who sounded a lot like Keith yelled, "FIRE!"

Everyone collectively decided that now would be the perfect time to yell a few things too. In the mess and confusion of students, Meghan found Charlotte and grabbed her hand.

"He did it!"

"I knew he would!" Charlotte said. "He's really good at destroying things."

"Come on," Meghan said. "We've got to do our part."

The two girls ran down the hall screaming and hollering with everyone else. Meghan knocked over a tall trash can and Charlotte hit one of the light switches, making the hall darker. The frightened masses were growing unstable. A girl tripped and her books flew forward, smashing the window on one of the classroom doors. The sound of breaking glass made everything even more chaotic.

"FIRE!" Meghan yelled.

It was the wrong time to yell. Meghan had failed to look behind her. Ms. Ratter, who had been running there, heard Meghan scream and grabbed her by the collar.

Everyone continued to run around Ms. Ratter and Meghan. Charlotte held back, hiding in the crowd.

"How do you know there's a fire?" Ms. Ratter demanded of Meghan.

"Fire?" Meghan echoed, trying hard to sound dumb.

"Come with me!"

Meghan knew she had been caught, and she wasn't going down without yelling a few more things. "FIRE! EVERYONE RUN FOR YOUR LIVES! RUN FOR YOUR LIVES!"

Ms. Ratter dragged Meghan away as fast as possible.

Charlotte tried to follow them, but she lost track of where they went as a chain of screaming girls ran through the hall and cut her off.

"All students to their dorms immediately," a voice over the loudspeaker ordered. "Immediately! To your dorms!"

This is very bad, Charlotte thought.

Meghan had been caught, and Witherwood was in turmoil.

CHAPTER 25

OPEN, HICKORY

"There, there" is a really nice thing to say when someone is hurting. Try it out. If a friend loses the remote, or drops something precious down a deep hole, pat them on the shoulder and say it. It's also useful to say if you're pointing to a building you don't know the name of, or if a bank robber is running down the street and you need to alert the authorities to where they are.

There, there!

It would have been nice if someone could have put a hand on Tobias's shoulder and said "there, there," but no one did. Instead, Fiddle pushed him and said, "You're probably in big trouble."

The two of them were near the back of Witherwood, hidden

in the trees and watching all the orderlies and staff streaming out of the school with buckets of water and wild expressions. They were running to the bonfire barn, which was burning like . . . well, a bonfire. The fire was intense and causing Tobias to worry about it spreading to the trees.

"If the trees catch fire, it could work its way to the school."

"Yep," Fiddle said.

"That's bad," Tobias reminded him. "Really bad."

From where they were, they could see the top of the fire and feel waves of heat. Smoke rose from the blaze like a dirty twister, sending ribbons of gray throughout the air.

"We've got to make it into the school and help students out the front," Tobias said. "This could turn into a good thing if everyone gets out okay."

Falling embers ignited a tree that was on the edge of the clearing. The tree began to burn. Flame from the tree hopped to another tree and then to another. A small chain of trees leading to the school lit up one after the other as if the fire were hopscotching its way to the back of Witherwood. Orderlies were hurling buckets of water at the trees, trying desperately to stop the flames from spreading.

A cedar tree burst into flame fifty feet from where Tobias and Fiddle were hiding. It crackled and popped, sending new embers up into the sky and drifting down toward the back wall of Witherwood.

"It's going to catch the school on fire!" Tobias yelled.

As he said it, a hairy shadow shot out of the trees and snapped the ember up into its mouth. Half a second later, the animal was gone.

"They're protecting the school," Fiddle said needlessly. "That's what they do."

Another ember drifted near, and once again, a Protector swooped in and snuffed it out. Three orderlies with a long hose were drenching the tree closest to the school with water.

"How do we get inside?!" Tobias asked Fiddle.

Fiddle ran farther into the trees along the side of Severe Hall with Tobias following behind him.

"There!" Fiddle yelled, pointing.

Tobias looked but couldn't tell what he was pointing at.

"That's where I broke my wrist when I was a little kid."

"We don't have time for reminiscing, Fiddle!"

"Right. Over here!"

Fiddle ran through a dozen more trees and stopped directly in front of one of the biggest on the mesa. It had a thick bark trunk and high branches covered with leaves that hung limply from every limb.

"This is the tree," Fiddle declared.

"What tree?" Tobias asked. "Is this where you stubbed your first toe? We're supposed to be going into Witherwood."

"You like to worry, don't you?"

"I like to live," Tobias retorted. "How do we get in?!"

Fiddle walked around the tree twice, staring at the trunk. He put his hands on the bark, feeling around for something.

"What...?"

Fiddle's fingers found what they were looking for. Digging into the crevices of the bark, he pulled and two large sections opened up like tall doors. Behind the bark, there was a very compact spiral staircase winding down through the roots of the tree.

"Wow," Tobias said.

"I hope I fit. I don't remember it being so tight."

"When did you last use this?"

"I think I was around seven."

"Where does it lead?"

"It goes a couple of places under the school. I just can't remember where."

"Why didn't we use this last time we came here?" Tobias said with frustration. "Or I could have used it today."

"I didn't know you wanted to. You seemed really excited to climb out the window."

Tobias stepped into the tree. The spiral stairs were narrow, but he was easily able to slip down them. Fiddle was a little bulkier, so his shoulders barely made it into the trunk. The stairs descended twenty steps and ended. Tobias pulled out his matches and struck one to see where he was. The light let him see that he was standing in a small cement room with an open tunnel that led south beneath Witherwood.

A draft of wind shot in from the tunnel and rattled up the spiral staircase, blowing out the match. Tobias struck another one.

"It's weird how dark some places are," Fiddle observed.

"Right," Tobias said. "It really is surprising to discover that it's dark underground."

"Exactly."

Tobias walked cautiously into the tunnel. His steps were slow and short, but in less than twenty of them, he reached a wall and the tunnel ran off in both directions. He thought about asking Fiddle which way they should go, but he knew the answer would only complicate things.

Tobias went left.

His match went out and he stopped to light another one.

"Why did you go this way?" Fiddle asked.

"I don't know," Tobias said, pulling the matches from his pocket. "Left felt right."

"Weird. I've always thought right felt right."

Tobias dropped the matches and swore. It was a mild swear-word. The kind of word that matched the mood of being in a dark tunnel while trying to save others and you accidentally drop your only source of light. Tobias went to his knees and felt around for the matches.

"What are all these tunnels for anyway?" he asked. "It seems like there might be more hidden behind the walls and floors of Witherwood than out in the open."

Fiddle dropped and helped him feel around.

"My uncle said that his father had a passion for secrets and that hidden tunnels and doors are necessary for certain secrets to flourish."

"Witherwood is baffling on so many levels," Tobias said. "I can't wait to tell people about it."

"It is remarkable," Fiddle agreed.

"Found them." Tobias grabbed the matches and stood up. His arms brushed against Fiddle as he did so. "Sorry."

"For what?" Fiddle asked, his voice coming from the opposite direction.

Tobias's heart did flips. He stepped backward and away from whatever had just brushed up against him. He nervously fiddled with the matches, trying to pull one out and strike it.

"What's happening?" Fiddle asked as Tobias pushed up against him.

Tobias struck a match.

There, staring at him, was a small animal. Its body was round

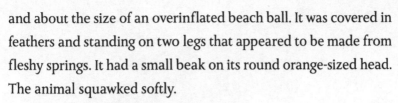

and about the size of an overinflated beach ball. It was covered in feathers and standing on two legs that appeared to be made from fleshy springs. It had a small beak on its round orange-sized head. The animal squawked softly.

"What is it?" Tobias asked.

"They're Whimms. They get in the tunnels sometimes," Fiddle answered. "I bet the fire's driving some down here."

"Is it harmful?"

"Not by itself," Fiddle said. "They don't attack unless they're clustered. My uncle Marvin has one he keeps on his shoulder as a pet."

"Capricious."

"Gesundheit," Fiddle said.

"That's what Lars must be."

"Lars?"

"Charlotte made friends with one. She named it Lars. It's weird because none of the animals up here seem to smell."

"They do at times," Fiddle said. "It used to be my job to clean up after one."

The Whimm in the tunnel squawked.

"So it won't hurt us?" Tobias asked, slowly backing up with Fiddle.

"I didn't say that. I said Whimms don't attack unless they're clustered."

The odd animal shivered and cocked its head to the side. It

made a sound similar to what one might imagine a turkey-chicken-monkey makes, and blinked its hairy eyelids. Something behind it made a different noise. Tobias lifted the match and the flame reflected off a dozen different pairs of eyes belonging to other Whimms in the tunnel.

"That's a cluster," Fiddle informed Tobias.

"Should we worry now?"

"Yes," Fiddle answered.

Tobias and Fiddle turned and ran. The match blew out and the darkness took over. Tobias kept his hands in front of him, desperately feeling for any obstacles or walls that might be in his way. The Whimms behind them were chirping and squawking. One hit up against Tobias's leg and bounced backward.

"Run faster!" Tobias yelled.

Fiddle gladly did as he was told.

CHAPTER 26

VISITORS

*Running in the dark is the worst. Running in the light is
no great treat, but it's way worse when you can't see anything. On your mark, get set, go run into a wall. Ready, set,
go fall into a hole. If you think about it, none of the Olympic
running games take place in underground tunnels. I believe
the dark plays a role in that decision.*

Tobias and Fiddle were not in the Olympics. They were
running in the dark somewhere beneath Severe Hall. It
was not a casual jog either; it was an all-out sprint as
they tried to get far away from the Whimms that were chasing
them.

Tobias's super smelling ability helped a little, but at the
moment, his legs were running faster than his nose could smell.

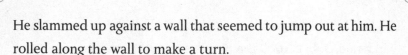
He slammed up against a wall that seemed to jump out at him. He rolled along the wall to make a turn.

"Watch out!"

The warning came too late. Fiddle hit the same wall and almost knocked Tobias over as he too was forced to turn.

"I'm okay," Fiddle yelled.

Tobias tripped on a set of stairs hidden in the dark. "Stairs!"

Fiddle crashed into the back of him.

Tobias quickly climbed the stairs. At the top was darkness. There was also a passageway behind the walls. Fiddle was up the stairs right behind Tobias.

"I don't think anything's following us anymore!"

Tobias wasn't taking chances. He kept running the one direction the passageway went. "You have no idea where this goes?"

"I had no idea it was this long."

Tobias ran with his hands out in front of him.

"Look," Tobias said.

Down the passageway there was a thin line of light at the bottom of the wall. When Tobias reached it, he could feel two metal handles that were attached to the wall at chest level. Fiddle bumped into Tobias again, coming to a stop.

"What is it?" Fiddle asked.

"There are a couple of handles on the wall."

Fiddle felt the handles. He tried to pull them, but nothing happened. Tobias took the handles and pushed. The lower part of the wall pushed out like a garage door opening. The two boys could see into a hall that was dark, but nowhere near as dark as the tunnel they had been running through. Somewhere off in the distance, an alarm was ringing.

They stepped into the hall and Tobias quickly closed the wall behind them. With it closed, there was no sign that the opening even existed. The hallway corridors were covered with wood paneling.

Time was of the essence, but Tobias pulled a pen from his pocket, rolled up the sleeve on his right arm, and quickly drew out what he could remember of the tunnel he had just been through. He rolled his sleeve down and put his pen away.

"Do you have any idea where we are?" he asked Fiddle.

"Witherwood?"

"Where in Witherwood?"

"I have no idea," Fiddle admitted.

The hallway they were in was narrow and cool. Down one direction there was nothing but darkness and the sound of people yelling. Down the other direction there was a single door with a plaque on it that read R44-ADMIN.

Tobias wanted to head toward the screaming, but a door with

the word ADMIN seemed like it might have a lot of answers hidden behind it.

"Come on," Tobias said. "Let's just see if this door is open."

It was.

Inside room R44 there were two desks and two rolling desk chairs. In the corner near the door stood a metal storage cabinet that was taller than Tobias by at least a foot. There were numerous bulletin boards on the walls, and all of them were covered with papers that had pins stuck through them. Tobias looked closely at some of the papers. Most of them were copies of want ads the school used to lure staff members to Witherwood.

ARE YOU DOWN AND OUT?

DO YOU NEED MONEY?

DO YOU THINK CHILDREN
NEED MORE INSTRUCTION?

DO YOU HATE ASKING QUESTIONS?

CAN YOU KEEP YOUR MOUTH SHUT?

WELL THEN, THIS MIGHT BE
THE JOB FOR YOU.

The two desks in the office were messy, but the bigger desk was the messiest. Papers and books were scattered across it and there were dozens of empty coffee cups tipped and stacked. On the floor there was a round rug with the fuzzy image of a cat on it. The room was dark, but some light shone from a very surprising source. On the corner of the big desk sat a small TV monitor that was glowing. The picture on the screen was the iron gate at the front of Witherwood.

"They have a security camera?" Tobias whispered.

"I think my uncle likes to know who's trying to come in."

Tobias sat down at the biggest desk and scooted the chair closer so he could properly stare at the monitor. Next to the monitor there was a red button on a little metal box. Near the button there was a phone. And by the phone there was an old-fashioned microphone.

Tobias studied the monitor and the iron gate he had first seen the night his father had abandoned them. His head hurt as he thought about all that had happened to them because of their dad.

"You know what I like about your sister?" Fiddle said as he stood behind Tobias.

"What?" Tobias asked, not sure he actually wanted to hear the answer.

"She has really good hearing. Like me."

"That's great," Tobias said, distracted and opening one of the desk drawers. "Wait. Why did you mention that?"

"Because I think I hear someone coming."

There was no time to complain about Fiddle's poor communication skills. Tobias stood up and moved to the metal storage cabinet. He opened the doors to find some yellow orderly jackets and a few buckets and brooms. He climbed into the cabinet, pulling Fiddle in with him. Tobias softly closed the metal doors as the office door opened. He could tell by the smell that it was Orrin.

"This isn't happening," Orrin said to himself. "This is not happening."

It was dark in the storage cabinet and Fiddle was breathing directly into Tobias's face. They heard Orrin pick up the telephone and push some buttons. Before he said anything, there was loud screaming from the other end.

"I know." Orrin finally got a word in edgewise. "Of course. We do think it was intentional. There have been two students caught. A boy and a girl."

More screaming on the other end.

"No," Orrin said, flustered. "It's not them. That was my first guess, but these are different children."

Screaming.

"If anyone tries to come into Witherwood, I will turn them

away. If by some outside chance they force their way in, we will be ready."

There was silence for a moment and then Orrin spoke again. "Actually, I can see on the monitor that someone is at the gate now." He sounded dejected.

"I'll handle this, Marvin. Just like I handled those children's father. Just like I handled the attacking Protectors. I'll handle this."

Tobias and Fiddle could hear Orrin hang up. Immediately following the phone being slammed down, they could hear him pick something up. There was a clicking noise and then Orrin began to make an announcement.

"Attention! There are visitors at the gate," he said calmly. "This is a code blue situation. Repeat, a code blue situation."

Orrin clicked off the microphone, banged a couple of drawers, and then scurried out of the room.

Tobias silently counted to twenty in his head before he opened the door of the metal cabinet. Orrin was gone, but on the monitor Tobias could see large fire trucks in front of the iron gate. He could also see some orderlies talking to the firefighters through the bars.

"They're not letting them in?" Tobias said, disgusted. "I can't believe it. This won't work if they can't get in."

"They don't like visitors here," Fiddle said, sounding like a friendly tour guide.

"We have to get to the gate and let them in."

Tobias ran out of the office and down the hall. At the other end of the hallway, there were metal bars that were locked tight with a very modern lock. Tobias shook the bars, trying to open them. He could see into another hall that had light at the end of it—light he couldn't reach.

"I don't think you're strong enough to break these bars," Fiddle said sadly. "I guess that's why the office wasn't locked. The bars would keep anyone out of that hallway."

"Yeah," Tobias lamented. "And now it's keeping us in."

Tobias turned and ran back to the wood panel they had come in through. He couldn't tell for sure which panel opened up, so he ran his fingers along the bottom of the wall, searching for the movable section.

"I think this is it," Tobias said. He tugged and pulled but the panel wouldn't budge. "It must have locked from the inside. I can't move it."

"Kick it," Fiddle suggested.

Tobias did some pretty hard kicking, but still nothing.

"Maybe there's a key to that metal door in the office?"

"Maybe," Fiddle said. "But I kind of doubt it."

Tobias frantically searched the desks in the office. Nothing. He looked at the bulletin boards, checking for keys that were hanging. Nothing. On the monitor, he could see Orrin at the closed iron gate. That was something.

The firefighters looked like they wanted in.

"If only we could open it from here," Tobias said.

"What's that red button?" Fiddle asked, pointing to the side of the monitor.

Tobias smiled. Memories of him standing in front of the iron gate and being buzzed in filled his thoughts. He glanced at the screen and saw the firefighters arguing with Orrin to be let in.

Tobias reached out and pushed the button.

The button made no noise in the office, but instantly he saw the firefighters on the screen reacting to something. They all stared at the gate as Orrin's jaw dropped. One firefighter with huge arms and a thick, wide mustache shoved the gate and it moved. All the firefighters began to push, and the gates swung open as Orrin hollered and yelled.

"They're in," Tobias said happily. "I can't believe it."

"Yeah, but we're still stuck," Fiddle reminded him.

Tobias looked at the screen. He could see Orrin looking up toward wherever the security camera was. He did not look happy. Orrin knew that someone had pushed the button, and Tobias and Fiddle were sitting ducks if they didn't find a way out.

"There has to be a key somewhere," Tobias said, pulling open desk drawers again and looking under papers and books.

"Actually there doesn't have to be," Fiddle said matter-of-factly.

Sadly, Fiddle was right.

CHAPTER 27

THE POWER OF PAPER AND PEN

Have you heard the news? If so, then you probably know what the word heard *means. Do you have a herd? If so, then you probably know what* herd *means. Do you know* Hurd? *If so, then you probably have shopped at that little shop on Fifth Avenue where Hurd Dillon is the night clerk.*

Wordplay is awful. (I hope no one heard that.)

Well, the staff of Witherwood had heard the announcement Orrin had made and *code blue* was being carried out in full force. All the students who had just been ordered to their dorms were now being herded back into six of the biggest classrooms. They were being sorted by age and commanded to sit down at desks where they were going to take a test.

Charlotte was placed in a large classroom with Ms. Ratter as her overseer. Every desk was filled, and every glaze-brained student was obediently staring at Ms. Ratter and waiting for her command.

"There has been too much commotion today," she finally said. "And due to that, we will be testing to remind you that you are students at a reform school and that is all. You need not concern yourself with animals or fire. We take your safety very seriously. In a moment, we may be visited by some people who have boldly entered our school to help put out a fire we had well under control. Do not speak to them. Keep your eyes on your test. If they ask you anything, tell them you are not supposed to be interrupted while testing. Understand?"

Every student in Charlotte's room nodded.

"Good," Ms. Ratter continued. "Raise your hand if you feel safe."

Everyone raised their hands.

Ms. Ratter and a few orderlies passed out the tests and pencils. Charlotte began checking off answers to make it look like she was doing what she was supposed to. She was physically sitting at her desk, but her mind was miles away, swimming in a pool of worry. She knew Meghan had been taken and she had seen no sign of Keith, or Tobias or Fiddle for that matter.

Ms. Gulp came charging into the classroom and walked

directly up to Ms. Ratter. She began talking in a loud whisper that was easy for Charlotte to hear.

"They've gotten through the gate," Ms. Gulp said.

"Orrin is a buffoon," Ms. Ratter hissed.

"That's completely true. He's like a pie in ointment."

"I believe you mean fly."

Ms. Gulp stared Ms. Ratter down for correcting her.

"Sorry."

Ms. Gulp nodded. "The fire is almost out. So hopefully our 'guests' won't be here long. If they come to the classrooms, act normal and thank them kindly for butting into our business."

"This day just keeps getting worse."

"Let's just get through this and we should be okay. Sheriff Pidge has promised he would smooth things out."

Charlotte trembled at the mention of Pidge.

"This lot of children better pay off," Ms. Gulp said. "They've been more trouble than the last ten years of students combined."

Ms. Gulp spotted Charlotte. "That reminds me, I haven't checked on the boy. I hope Orrin has him locked in his room." She spun around and marched back out of the classroom.

Charlotte didn't have a moment to waste. Ms. Gulp was going to look for Tobias, and if anyone from outside of Witherwood did check on her classroom, she needed to be ready. She carefully tore off a square of paper from the last sheet of her test. As quietly as she could, she wrote some tiny words on the paper.

Ms. Ratter looked up from her desk and then looked back down.

Charlotte folded the square piece of paper and hid it in her lap. She was hoping to have the courage to speak up if a firefighter came in. If she couldn't, she would slip the note into the fire-fighter's hand or pocket.

The students continued to check off answers on their tests. There was no clock on the wall and it felt like time had stopped. The school had been so noisy and out of control earlier, and now it was silent. There was nothing but the sound of pencils scratching against paper as everyone checked off boxes to questions like, *How many children does it take to form a club?*

The answers were as ridiculous as the questions.

A. 2

B. 5

C. *Clubs are a bad idea.*

D. *Children are too uneducated to answer questions like this.*

Just as Charlotte felt certain that nobody from the outside world was going to check on their classroom, she heard the door open, and a fireman with big arms and a large mustache stepped in. He was wearing fire gear and big boots. On his back was a pack, and he had a helmet on his head with an open face guard. He smiled the kind of smile that only someone who didn't live at Witherwood would be capable of.

"Hello," he said.

All the students continued to take their test.

"Come in," Ms. Ratter said. "We feel so grateful for you all. I'm sorry the students are testing. They are normally much more talkative than this."

Charlotte didn't look up, but from the corner of her eye, it looked like Ms. Ratter was blushing.

"I'm sorry to interrupt," the fireman said. "I just wanted to let you know that the fire is out and that there's no danger now."

"That's wonderful."

Ms. Ratter walked down the aisle closer to the tall fireman.

"We were lucky you didn't need to evacuate the school," he said.

Charlotte didn't feel lucky at all. She also knew that she had to speak up.

"All right, then," the fireman said as he turned to leave. "Have a nice day."

It was now or never.

"Help," Charlotte said from the corner of her mouth.

Ms. Ratter and the fireman turned around quickly and looked at the class.

"Excuse me?" the fireman said. He glanced at Ms. Ratter. "Did you hear that?"

"Hear what?"

The fireman came farther into the classroom and began to walk down an aisle two rows away from Charlotte. He looked at the students as they took their tests. Ms. Ratter walked down Charlotte's row, giving all the children her evilest stink eye possible. She stopped right next to Charlotte's desk and put her right hand on Charlotte's shoulder and her left hand on the shoulder of the girl next to her.

"Did any of you students say something?" Ms. Ratter asked so sweetly that it almost made Charlotte sick.

Not a single student uttered a single peep.

Charlotte knew the note was in her lap, so she leaned forward to keep it hidden. Ms. Ratter took her hand off Charlotte's shoulder and began to walk back up the aisle.

"Maybe I'm just hearing things," the fireman said. "I guess it's been a long day." He too turned around and began to walk to the door.

Charlotte's heart sank. She wanted to yelp again, but she was terrified of getting caught. She had the note, but the fireman was two aisles over, walking away.

Without even realizing it, her hands began to quickly fold the small piece of paper beneath her desk. It was a long shot, but it had been tadpoles that got her into Witherwood. Now it was Charlotte's hope that a small paper frog might get her out. Charlotte finished the frog in a flash. She looked up and saw Ms. Ratter walking with her back turned to her. She sized up the fireman and the large backpack he had on. There were all sorts of open pockets and parts. There was no time to even think about how impossible what she was about to do was.

Charlotte put the little origami frog on the corner of her desk. She aimed and applied the perfect amount of pressure. She let go, and the little frog hopped over the row of children next to her and landed on top of the fireman's backpack.

Charlotte wanted to cheer, but right after it landed, the frog slid off the backpack and fell directly into the large right boot the fireman was wearing.

Nobody had noticed.

Ms. Ratter opened the door for the fireman and he left the room. As soon as he was gone, Ms. Ratter charged down the aisle, heading directly for Charlotte. Charlotte thought about screaming, but Ms. Ratter reached out and grabbed the ear of a girl next to her.

"Think you can make noises?" Ms. Ratter barked. "You're going to see Marvin."

Ms. Ratter pulled the wrong girl out of the classroom and turned her over to an orderly.

Charlotte felt awful, but since the girl's brain was still gooey, Marvin's voice wouldn't change things too much for her.

It seemed impossible, but Charlotte knew that she might have made contact. She couldn't wait to tell Tobias.

CHAPTER 28

TUNED IN

Blue is a color. If you are colored blue, you may be navy, baby, or dark. Blue is also a feeling. If you feel blue, you are sad, melancholy, or down in the dumps. Ralph was blue, the glow of the TV giving his body a light blue hue. He also felt blue—all his searching and wondering and looking, and still no real clue as to who he was.

Ralph blew his nose, which is a different kind of blue altogether.

"Here," Sam said, offering Ralph a small trash bin to throw his tissue in.

Ralph took the trash bin, threw his tissue away, and then set it by the side of the couch. He felt a cold coming on. He ran his hands through his hair and cleared his throat. The two of them were sitting in the front room of Sam's three-story town house. The TV was showing a commercial for dog food. Sam was on the couch about five feet from Ralph. Both of them were tired and depressed from searching yet coming up empty.

"Maybe you should consider taking me up on my offer," Sam said.

"What offer?"

"I'll help you get a taxi to drive. The police are always auctioning off their old vehicles. You can make a few bucks and you'd be in charge of picking out the air freshener for your vehicle. Plus, you get to learn the city really well. Did you know there are two streets named Tony?"

Ralph shook his head.

"Yeah, and a cul-de-sac called Wilbur's Circle."

"Wow."

"Ah, you're just saying that," Sam complained. "I can tell you don't mean it."

"Sorry," Ralph apologized. "I just don't know what to do next."

"Drive a taxi," Sam insisted. "Look what it's gotten me." Sam motioned to his couch and house and TV. "I know car salesmen who don't have a TV this big."

"Driving a taxi is a fine profession, but I don't want to just give up looking. Not yet. I need to know who I am."

"You wouldn't be giving up, you would be living the dream while figuring things out. Think about it...."

Sam stopped talking, because it was apparent that his friend had stopped listening. Ralph was staring at the TV screen with a look of shock and awe.

"Turn it up," Ralph said.

Sam grabbed the remote and turned up the volume. On the screen, there was footage of a large fire burning on top of a mesa. A news helicopter was circling the mesa and filming the dying fire. A TV anchorwoman was talking as the helicopter filmed.

"What we know at the moment is that the fire is contained. There are many firefighters now on the premises, but they had some problem getting to the fire due to its location. There are no reports of fatalities, and only one injury occurred when someone running from the fire slipped and hit his head on a urinal. The victim was treated on the premises and released. The building on fire is said to be a barn where the school kept equipment and yard supplies...."

"You've got to be kidding," Ralph whispered. "There has to be something to this."

"It's another weird coincidence. Remember, that photo of those kids was a dead end," Sam warned. "I can't imagine what a fire means."

"It means we're going back there."

"That's sort of what I thought it might mean," Sam admitted.

"That weird school up on that weird mesa has some answers."

"Or," Sam said, trying to keep things in perspective, "hear me out—it could mean that weird school up on that weird mesa has problems, and we'd be smart not to worry about them."

"One more look," Ralph begged. "Let's just give it one more look. If it comes to nothing, then we cross it off for good."

Sam sighed. "I guess we can make one last visit. You know, it costs a lot to drive out there. Gas ain't cheap."

"I'll pay you back double someday."

"Fair enough. And I do like the smell of fire."

They both jumped up and headed out.

CHAPTER 29

DOWN BUT NOT OUT

Tobias and Fiddle had kicked and pulled at every wood panel in the hallway, and not a single one of them would budge. The one they had come through originally was locked. They also hadn't found keys in the office to open the metal bars at the end of the hall.

After rummaging through the desks, they had tried to put things back like they had found them, so if and when they were discovered, it wouldn't look like they had gone through stuff.

"Are you sure you don't know of some other secret passage that leads away from here?" Tobias asked Fiddle again. "I don't want to get caught and then have you say you knew of a way but I didn't ask correctly."

"I've never been in this part of the school," Fiddle said. "I wasn't aware this was here."

"Well, then I don't know how we're getting out of this," Tobias said. "I only hope someone who came because of the fire will free us all."

"Um," Fiddle said. "It looks like people are leaving."

Tobias stared at the monitor on the large desk. He could see fire trucks exiting Witherwood through the iron gate. He hung his head between his legs and took a couple of really deep breaths.

"It's not all bad," Fiddle said, trying to cheer him up. "I don't know how long I've been alive, but I've never seen anyone try as hard as you to change things here. Most of the students I've met or spied on were unable to think for themselves. You and your sister are so different."

"It doesn't mean anything," Tobias whispered. "I failed again. Orrin will find us here and he'll know we buzzed the firefighters in. He'll probably also figure out that it was me who started the fire. Then he'll take me to that pool, and tomorrow I'll be ninety years old."

"Time does fly," Fiddle said, as if he were reminiscing about the good old days.

"It shouldn't fly that fast."

"It'll be okay, Tobias."

It was weird for Tobias to hear Fiddle use his name. Most of the time he felt as if Fiddle didn't really know he was real.

"Things are different this time," Fiddle said. "I'm not the same person I used to be. I know that my uncle needs to be stopped and I want to be one of the people to stop him. They might catch us in here, but I'll play dumb and I'll find your sister and we'll break the chain of misery that my uncle is forging."

"That's not a bad line," Tobias said. "Keith would be proud."

"Who's Keith?"

"He's one of the students who's going to help us bring Wither-wood down."

"He sounds nice."

"There are so many questions I wish I had answers to."

Fiddle scratched at his arm and clicked his teeth.

"You okay?" Tobias asked.

"I know someone," he blurted out. "He might be able to help."

"Who?" Tobias asked suspiciously.

"I'm not supposed to talk about him. He knows everything and he lives beneath the square building."

"With Marvin?"

"No, Uncle Marvin spends most of his time in the square room, but he actually sleeps in a big fancy place in East Hall."

"So someone else lives in a room under the square building?"

"It's not really a room," Fiddle said, acting embarrassed. "It's more like a big cage."

Tobias stared at Fiddle. He had no idea who he was talking about.

"There's someone in a prison cell under the square building?"

"What?" Fiddle asked, scratching nervously at his right arm.

"Fiddle," Tobias said kindly, "is there someone beneath the square building who can help us?"

Fiddle looked at the ground. "He doesn't like Marvin at all."

"That's a good thing in my book."

"My uncle said he wants to ruin everything."

"Another good thing."

"He's my dad."

"You have a dad who's alive?" Tobias asked, dumbfounded.

"I'm not allowed to see him," Fiddle said. "I haven't seen him in years. He and my uncle don't get along."

Tobias grabbed a pen off the desk and wrote himself a note. He folded the small piece of paper and crammed it deep into his pocket.

"What are you doing?" Fiddle asked.

"If your uncle catches me and speaks to me again, I want to remember your dad."

"I do too," Fiddle said.

"We've got to get out of here," Tobias said with new resolve. "And let's hope that fire has made at least one outsider curious enough to really check things out."

"I'm hoping for three."

Tobias pulled his hand out of his pocket. There were bits of the secret ingredient on his fingers.

"Any idea what this is?" he said, holding his hand in front of Fiddle's face.

Fiddle sniffed. "Nope, but my dad probably knows."

"We need your dad."

"Tell me about it."

"We need to take down this school."

"No, really," Fiddle said. "Tell me about my dad."

Tobias took a few moments to tell his friend about a person he had never met, but also about a person who might actually have some answers.

CHAPTER 30

EVENING THE SCORE

When the fire was dead, the firelighters left without ever knowing what the true tragedy was. The iron gates were closed, and with that, any hope of happiness was lost. Students were ushered from the classrooms and returned to their dorms. There they would be put until things were sorted out.

Charlotte marched through the smoky gardens with everyone else, heading toward Severe Hall. In front of her, she could see, and hear, Orrin and Ms. Gulp walking and talking. They were both very loud.

"I don't know who did it," Orrin said angrily. "In fact, I'm on my way to see if I can find out."

"What a mess," Ms. Gulp growled. "This day has been cupful."

"I think you mean *awful*," Orrin corrected her. "Awful indeed, but we're lucky to have dodged true disaster. Now we just need to speed things up. As you know, fire or no fire, the new recruits will be coming shortly."

"Yes, *as I know*," Ms. Gulp snapped. "Stop telling me things I'm already aware of."

Orrin broke away from Gulp and headed off in another direction.

Charlotte watched him disappear into the waves of children. Her head was clear, but her heart was foggy. There were so many things *she* didn't know. There were people she was worried about, and a brother she wished were here. She kept looking around carefully for any sign of him. It was quite possible that he had gone unnoticed and had not been caught. If Tobias had been captured or hurt, Charlotte didn't think she could go on.

Tobias is fine, she thought over and over in an attempt to comfort herself. *Tobias is fine.*

As Charlotte moved with the other students, she looked around the gardens carefully. The air was smoky and burned her eyes, but even as they watered, she saw something.

"Lars?" she whispered in amazement.

Up ahead, in the branches of a cottonwood tree, Charlotte noticed a spot of orange. Her heart beat wildly as she looked around, wondering if anyone else could see the tiny creature.

Nobody seemed to.

The students Charlotte was walking with were only a few feet from the tree. More than anything, she wanted to reach out and grab Lars. But he was too high to reach. She wished for a net to scoop him up and take him with her. But she didn't have one.

As she got closer to the tree, Charlotte could see Lars staring directly at her and shaking excitedly.

She smiled at him and his little round head bobbed.

Her heart broke even further. Witherwood was a place with so few bright spots, and now she was having to walk right by one of the only things she cared about here.

How many times can life be unfair?

Well, fortunately for Charlotte, life was looking to even the score a bit. As she passed by the tree, Lars jumped and, in one swift blur, flew into Charlotte's hands. Without a moment's hesitation, she pushed the tiny creature into her skirt pocket and pulled down her shirt to cover him up as much as possible.

Charlotte's heart was having a fit. She looked around, but once again nobody seemed to have noticed.

Charlotte carefully patted her pocket, and for the first time in a while, she smiled. The smoke filled Charlotte's eyes, but she cried for a different reason.

Sometimes happiness is surprising.

CHAPTER 31

LOST

Lost *is a sad little word. It makes me feel, well, lost. It has very few word friends to make it look better. Follow up* lost *with words like keys, time, love, antidote, happiness, money, or wallet, and you'll find little to celebrate. I lost a bet once, a dog twice, and an argument about turnips more times than I can count. Lost treasure is pretty exciting, but only if you've found it. If you haven't found it yet, then it's just lost. There's not much to be happy about when all is lost, and there's even less to rejoice about when a lost cause causes you to lose sleep.*

I lost where I'm going with this.

Oh yes, Ralph Eggers was lost. He knew where he was, but his life was adrift. Lost at sea like a ship on a stormy bay. His only hope at the moment was to return to Witherwood and find out if the fire meant anything. During the drive from the city into the lonely desert, they had been able to witness small clouds of black smoke high in the air. You couldn't see the mesa from the city, because it was too far, but the smoke was visible. Now, as they got closer, it seemed as if the sky was colored gray from smoke.

Sam took the ranch exit and turned onto the highway.

"I don't think this fire will have answers," Sam said.

"Well, then I'll be just as lost as ever."

When they reached the Witherwood sign, there were dozens of cars and news vans parked along the side of the road. In the distance, the tall mesa stood straight up with a crown of gray.

The turnoff to Witherwood was blocked by three police cars that had their lights flashing. A single police officer was standing in front of the vehicles. Sam pulled up and rolled his window down.

"Road's closed," the officer informed them.

"I can see that," Sam said. "What happened?"

"Just a fire. Probably caused by lightning. It's all under control now."

"Lightning?" Ralph asked. "The sky's clear."

"Except for the black smoke up there," Sam added.

"It's a desert," the police officer said. "Sometimes you get dry lightning. Move on."

"There's no way we could just drive up and see if we can help?" Ralph asked. "We were supposed to meet with Orrin."

"Really?" the officer said, stepping closer to the taxi. He leaned down and sniffed. The name tag on his uniform read SHERIFF PIDGE. "I think Orrin's got a lot on his plate at the moment. So why don't you two just move along."

"Can I ask you one last question?" Ralph asked.

"Quickly," Sheriff Pidge replied.

"What do you know about that school up there?"

"It's one of the finest," he answered. "First-rate staff doing remarkable things to reform children in need of reforming. The world would be better off if there were more institutions like Witherwood."

"It sounds like you work for them," Sam said snidely.

Sheriff Pidge stepped even closer. "Well, I don't. I work for the good people of this county, and I'm beginning to wonder if it wouldn't serve the people well to take you two down to the station and let you spend a little time thinking about the proper way to speak to a sheriff."

"Really?" Sam said heated. "Why—"

"That's okay," Ralph interrupted. "We'll be on our way. Come on, Sam."

Sam reluctantly pulled away and continued down the

highway past the other cars and spectators. He was hot under the collar from how the sheriff had talked to him, so he drove in silence for a mile as he cooled off.

"You give some people a little authority and they turn into jerks," Sam finally said.

To the right, they could see the mesa in the distance and smoke in the air. Sam sighed and pulled over at an abandoned rest stop.

"I don't think the bathrooms work here," Ralph said.

"I didn't stop for the facilities. I figure since we're out here we might as well watch the smoke. Maybe that ignorant cop will leave and we can try to go up again."

Ralph and Sam got out of the taxi and sat on the front of the car, staring into the distance. The mesa looked pale under the cloud of swirling smoke that was positioned above it like a halo.

"I hate to say it," Sam said, "but I really think this school has nothing to do with you. It just happens to be in the area where you were found, so we keep finding connections. The subconscious mind is weird that way. It's like when you say you never see any brown cars, and then for the next few days, you see a ton of brown cars. We're just seeing Witherwood because it was there."

"I think you might be right," Ralph said. "Besides, if there was a connection, why wouldn't they know me?"

"Right, you're a memorable guy."

Three fire trucks coming from the direction of Witherwood

pulled off the highway and into the overgrown parking lot of the abandoned rest stop. A handful of firefighters jumped off the trucks.

Okay, I don't know about you, but I feel very hopeful right now. I mean, Ralph and Sam and a bunch of fire-fighters are all hanging out in the parking lot of the abandoned rest stop. The very same rest stop that Tobias and Charlotte emerged from after their first escape attempt from Witherwood. All that is needed is for someone to bust into the restroom and discover the hidden entrance to the tunnel that will take them to Witherwood.

"The rest stop is boarded up," Sam said in a friendly tone.

"Thanks," a firefighter with thick arms and a large mustache replied. "We just need to set our gear better."

"So the fire's out?" Ralph asked.

"Yes, there's a few men still wetting things down with garden hoses, but the fire's out. It was just one building filled with flammable things."

"How did it start?" Sam asked.

"One of the workers accidentally started it when he was trying to fix an old tractor. We'll be sending a fire inspector out to make sure that's the case."

"Hope he can get in," a second firefighter said.

"They definitely don't enjoy others coming onto their school grounds," Captain Mustache said. "And that sheriff, he's worse than all of them. We couldn't even pack our trucks correctly because he insisted we leave."

"If it's the same sheriff we met, I don't care for him either," Sam said, spitting.

"There are a few more trucks still coming down the mesa. We're actually stationed all the way back in town. We were out here supervising some controlled burns when we spotted the smoke. It's weird how some folks just don't want help."

The firefighters strapped things tighter to their trucks and wound up their hoses properly, while Ralph and Sam watched the mesa. A couple of the firefighters started talking about going to get something to eat. One mentioned a certain place back in the city.

Ralph didn't mean to eavesdrop, but he did.

"Excuse me," Ralph said with excitement, interrupting two firefighters. "What did you just say?"

"We were just talking about getting something to eat and drink. We usually meet up after a job to unwind."

"Sure, sure," Ralph said. "That makes sense, but where did you say you were going to eat?"

"It's just a dive down in the industrial district. Cheap food and drinks. Not many people know about it."

"But what's it called?" Ralph was beside himself.

"Burkenfield's."

Ralph looked at Sam. "Isn't that the name Orrin gave us?"

Sam nodded.

Sam looked at Ralph. "Hungry?"

"More like hopeful," Ralph replied. "It's a lead, right?"

"As good as any we've had before."

The two got directions from the firefighters and quickly abandoned the rest stop. And for a moment, Ralph felt a little less lost.

CHAPTER 32

FOUND

Most people want to grow up to be something. Some people aspire to be astronauts or presidents. Some want to own their own landscaping business or fireworks stand. I was recently interviewed by a woman who wanted to grow up to interview authors who wrote things about Witherwood. It was very satisfying to see her achieve her goal. Another popular thing to want to be is a firefighter. They are known for bravery and heroics and the occasional charity bake sale.

Mike Mann was born to be a firefighter.

As a child, he put out a fire at the old mill. As a teenager, he put out a fire at the new high school, and as an adult, he put out fires at buildings of all ages.

He was known as Fireman Mike, and he felt like he was doing just what he was born to do. Of course, occasionally there were fires that made him think. Like the time the city pool burned down, or the fire on top of the mesa he had just helped put out.

Mike and his crew had almost not been allowed on the premises. Then they were almost not allowed to drive their trucks to the back of the school where the fire was. And after they finally got to the fire and put it out, they were quickly escorted off the premises by the local police. Now he was standing in the overgrown parking lot of a boarded-up rest stop winding up his hose and securing his truck.

"That was a weird one," Mike said to another firefighter, named Jeff.

Jeff was new, but he was able to recognize what an odd job they had just been through. "Yeah, I don't think we were welcome. And I have to say, where that school is located doesn't make it any more normal. I've never seen anything like that."

Both firefighters looked into the distance at the mesa, which still had light smoke encircling the top of it. They could see a helicopter flying overhead.

"It might be a weird school, but the kids were well behaved," Mike said as he removed one of his boots and put on a regular shoe.

"I guess so. I hated school and could never sit still. Those kids looked like they were professional students."

Mike took off his other boot. He was about to look inside when another news copter flew overhead.

"People love fires," Jeff said.

"That's the truth." Mike tossed his boot into the truck and slipped on his other shoe. "Let's go to Burkenfield's."

"Did you think it was odd how excited those two guys at the rest stop were about it?"

"Yeah, but it's been a weird day."

Mike and his crew got back into their trucks and drove off.

If you're like me, you're a bit bothered that Mike didn't look into his boot and notice the note Charlotte slipped him. I mean, the chapter is called "Found," and that would have been the perfect thing for Mike to find. I want the world to know that I think there are few professions more noble and brave, and that I am grateful for all firefighters do, but in this instance, I'm just a little disappointed.

Actually, it's more than that.

I MIGHT ADD

I want to believe the world is good. I want to believe that behind every closed door there's a clear mystery that ends in a happy way. I want to see blue skies and bright stars and double rainbows out my window. I want the people I care about to be showered in success, and I would like the people I don't care about to know I wish them well—in the sense that I wish they would fall down into a well. That seems harsh, but what I didn't tell you is that at the bottom of the well they will have ample time to think about what they have done and change their ways for good.

You see, all's well that ends well.

Well, this isn't the end. Yes, things are a bit dicey. Patrick and Meghan are facing Marvin's voice again. Archie is resting, but he is most certainly not himself. You might be surprised to know where Sue and Keith ended up after the fire. Well, that's one surprise that will have to wait. Let's hope it's a good one.

And Ralph and Sam are following a lead that is based on a word Orrin just tossed out.

Burkenfield.

Charlotte is pretending to be dumb and she is alone. And Tobias and Fiddle are trapped in a hallway trying to find a way out before Orrin returns and finds them.

Dicey indeed.

Everyone experiences difficulty in life. We all have good days and bad days. On some days, we're lucky just to have good hours. And on other days, we are quite fortunate to simply have a few seconds of hope.

Well, if Patrick and Keith and Meghan and Ralph and Sam and Charlotte and Fiddle and Tobias knew what Fireman Mike was eventually going to find in his boot, they would all be in for more than a few seconds of hope.

I believe I can safely say, all is not lost.

And if Orrin and Marvin and Ms. Ratter and Ms. Gulp knew what Mike was going to discover, they might all be in for more than a few seconds of misery.

I love it when the good people find hope and the bad people find the loss they deserve.

WITHERWOOD REFORM SCHOOL

BOOK 3

THE NEW ORDER

Things are changing rapidly at Witherwood—the institution is being challenged, and a new order has been set in place. Tobias and Charlotte find their hands full of possibility and danger as outside forces seek to destroy their very lives and quiet the growing rebellion. Their only hope is to discover the source of Witherwood's power and put an end to the experiments. It will take some considerable risks, but Tobias and Charlotte are willing to gamble all they have in an attempt to blow open the secrets and set Witherwood free.

The way is clear; the means are ...ing
In glow of day or on the night sea.
Repent, repair, and wish them well.
Too soon to tell, too soon to tell.

Class 2b

Sis's new room?

We

A

Class 2a

Labs?

Fiddle's room (trust him?)

Severe Hall

R44- Admin (important?)

Library

Goat tapestry entrance

Grounds Keeper's

E a

Class 2d

Boiler room Meeting spot!

Store room

Watch the darkness!

Look